Pilgrim's Pie
A Time-Travel Thanksgiving Romance
By: Jodi Chow

PILGRIM'S PIE

First edition. May 13, 2024.

Copyright © 2024 Jodi Chow.

ISBN: 979-8224024872

Written by Jodi Chow.

Chapter One- Harvest Talisman

AUTUMN ARRIVED WITH a whispered sigh. Leaves, like fire, set the trees aglow in the sky. A silent dance of fresh air and foliage was taking place in the background of natural modern rhythms. The days were short and crisp, barely escaping the ever-present effects of global climate change. The Tautog family long awaited this time of the year. Cape Cod unveils its timeless beauty, a masterpiece of nature's artistry with a futuristic twist. The air, still kissed by the Atlantic's gentle breeze, carries a hint of nostalgia, mingled with the promise of a changing world.

As the leaves began their graceful descent, a kaleidoscope of colors adorned the landscape. Trees, resilient to the shifting climate, wore their vibrant plumes with pride. Brilliant reds, intense and lively oranges, and golden yellows painted the horizon.

The coastline, where rocky shores meet violent waves, remained an ever-present sanctuary. Though touched by the rising tides, Cape Cod stood resolute, embracing the dance of the waves as they caressed its shores. Seagulls, now accompanied by futuristic drones, glided effortlessly overhead, harmonizing the old and new.

Amidst the dunes and marshes, wildlife persisted, adapting to a changing environment. Here, where the salt marshes met the sea, the call of migratory birds echoed with determination, and the whispers of endangered species constantly reminded humanity of the shared responsibility to sustain and nurture the very essence of life.

In this futuristic autumn, Cape Cod preserved its heritage while embracing innovation. Solar panels adorned the rooftops of historic homes, and wind turbines rose like modern sentinels, harnessing the power of the ever-present Atlantic winds. Sustainable practices and eco-conscious communities were the guiding stars, and only remaining backbone, from a technologically-focused era that flailed under the pressure of a society crippled by vices. There was, however, a newly reinvigorated energy that was guiding people to an even more prosperous future.

As the sun sets on this Cape Cod of 2050, a sense of hope and resilience filled the air. The landscape, the past and the future, entwine in a timeless embrace, where nature's beauty remained the steadfast heartbeat of the coastal paradise.

Philip stood at the helm of his electric boat, guiding it gracefully towards the weathered, sun-bleached dock at Buzzards Bay. His physical appearance bore the marks of a life closely intertwined with the sea. He stood with a proud and sturdy posture, his physique reflecting a combination of strength and grace that came from thirty years of working on the water.

Philip's skin was a warm, sun-kissed bronze, an intriguing map of countless days spent under the coastal sun. His jet-black hair, ruffled by the sea breeze, fell to his shoulders, and a few stray locks clung to his forehead. His hair was slightly damp, as a few droplets from the ocean's spray had found their way to his tanned face.

His deep brown eyes held an ocean's depth of wisdom, reflecting an intimate understanding of the bay's ebbs and flows. The lines at the corners of his eyes and around his mouth told stories of many seasons spent on the water, revealing a life marked by both challenges and rewards.

A worn and faded blue fishing shirt clung to his muscular frame, soaked in a mixture of sweat and saltwater. He wore faded jeans and rugged boots, each scuffed and seasoned by years of navigating rocky shores and sandy beaches. He liked his boots durable and mundane so as not to invoke jealousy from his fellow fishermen. Understated was a great word to describe Philip's style. His mother hated that he looked like a pauper, but appreciated his approach to living a humble life.

The air of the bay was infused with the scent of brine and seaweed, and Philip's presence seemed to blend seamlessly with this coastal environment. His very spirit was one with nature and his fellow man as he worked. His hands, rough and calloused, wore the signature of a dedicated fisherman, strong and dexterous from years of handling nets, lines, and fish. With a strong and lean frame, Philip embodied a deep connection to the sea, a heritage passed down through generations of his Wampanoag ancestors.

As the boat glided effortlessly onto the worn wooden planks of the dock, the electric motor hummed with a quiet, environmentally-friendly power. Philip's eyes sparkled with the satisfaction of a successful day on the water. He had been fishing from sunrise to sunset, drawing from the age-old wisdom of his people and harnessing modern technology. He appreciated the modern conveniences his ancestors did not possess, and almost wondered if he was relying too heavily upon these creature comforts.

In the cooler, nestled on the boat's deck, glistened an impressive catch of the day. Glistening in the late afternoon sun were silvery bluefish, vibrant mackerel, and hefty striped bass. Philip had an uncanny knack for finding the best spots and luring in the finest catches, a skill that set him apart in this sustainable fishing trade.

He carefully began unloading his catch, preparing for the evening market where he would sell his bounty to local seafood vendors the next day. Philip was not just a fisherman; he was an advocate for responsible fishing practices. He knew the importance of preserving the bay's delicate eco-system and balancing the needs of his community with the health of the environment. His vendors looked forward to his domineering personality and exuberance for a clean and healthy life. The vendors knew with an air of authority that Philip's fish were the best around. Every time Philip met with the local vendors, he wondered if his mother was right. *Maybe I should upgrade my clothes for showmanship.* He thought to himself. He didn't have time to second guess himself today. He also knew he had to get home as soon as possible.

As the sun dipped below the horizon, casting a warm, golden glow over the Cape Cod bay, Philip stood proud, embodying the harmonious coexistence of tradition and innovation, a steward of the region, ensuring that his people's way of life would endure for generations to come.

In the waning light, Philip's hurried silhouette danced across the weathered planks of the dock. The urgency in his movements betrayed a quiet anticipation as he raced to secure the boat, the rhythmic lap of the bay's waves echoing his haste.

With eyes fixed on the horizon, Philip's strong shoulders flexed as he deftly tied the mooring lines, securing the vessel with practiced precision. The vessel moaned its secrets to him, urging him home to the heartwarming embrace of tradition and family.

For tonight, Weetamoo, his mother, wove culinary magic from the memories of generations past. She conjured the aromas of a traditional feast, the very essence of their ancestral connection. The promise of a nourishing meal, rich in heritage, tugged at Philip's soul.

His heart quickened as he imagined the warm glow of their home, the intricate smells of sweet and savory, and the chorus of voices retelling stories of their people. Philip knew that in his mother's hands, the ingredients of the past would harmonize with the flavors of the present.

Philip's footfalls resonated with purpose as he raced against the setting sun, determined not to be late for the ritual that bound their family to this time and place. For in Weetamoo's kitchen, the past and the future converged, just as they did on the shifting tides of Buttermilk Bay.

Philip was torn from his thoughts as his e-boat almost scraped the dock. He was always responsible with his assets given the fact that he did not want to disappoint his father or cause his family any harm. Philip may have his own electric boat, but his father had fleets of ships at his disposal. Frustrated with the time it was taking to properly moor the boat (RobEE he called her), Philip began feeling lightheaded. He decidedly slowed down and methodically got the task of storing the boat appropriately completed. Minutes later, he was in his Tesla and on his way home.

Philip was always inspired by the way Metacomet-or Meta for short- made sure his family was taken care of. Meta was Philip's father and the descendent of the original Chief Metacomet. Metacomet's father was Chief Massasoit. Massasoit was the sachem that made peaceful alliances with the pilgrims from the Mayflower. Tradition had it that hundreds of years ago, a nobleman from the Old World found favor on Philip's great-great grandfather. Philip's family was originally known for being kind and hospitable, and the nobleman noticed that and wanted to celebrate the peaceful nature of his family, so he bequeathed Philip's family 5,000 British pounds. His great-great grandfather decided to continue his tribe's fishing legacy, and soon, Tautog Enterprises was formed.

Within the entanglements of modern society, the Tautog family stood as a steadfast pillar, a bridge that connected the screams and trials of history with the cadence of the present. They considered themselves the gatekeepers, their stories living legends, where the past and the present coalesced in harmonious resonance.

Amidst a world of Native American and English adversaries, the Tautog family's unity, like the sturdy hull of a vessel, kept them afloat. Their roots intertwined with the soil of ancestral lands, and their branches reached toward the promise of the future. The Tautlogs were no strangers to opposition, adversity, or entrapments. They used their minds, hearts, and souls to fight off enemies in a dance of love. They submitted when necessary and stood strong when needed for centuries. Their dance was one to emulate.

Their matriarchs and patriarchs, custodians of ancient wisdom, passed down through unbelievable tales and treasured relics. They were the beacons that illuminated the path of traditions, the keepers of languages that ached with the laughter and laments of generations past.

Through the turbulence of history's tides, the Tautog family had remained unyielding. Their resilience, like the ever-flowing stream, carved a steady course through the challenges of time. They carried within them the legacy of endurance, common purpose, and progress.

The Tautog estate stood as a magnificent structure and a timely product of a family's enduring legacy, nestled amidst the embrace of nature's grandeur. With a long and winding driveway that meandered through lush woodlands, it was as if the very earth itself beckoned visitors toward its welcoming embrace. Philip thought the same as he gaily drove his white EV through the course.

At last, Philip was home and enjoying the breathtaking view of his family's compound once again. The exterior of the mansion, adorned with intricate wood carvings of fish, reflected the family's profound connection to the sea, each carving a masterpiece worth admiring.

The Tautog estate was not merely a residence; it was a place where time itself stood still, where traditions murmured in the breezes that rustled the leaves. Philip parked his car and joyfully ran inside where his mother awaited him in the grand kitchen.

Gleaming quartz countertops embraced the colors of cranberry bogs and sandy shores, as sunlight bathed the space through large, panoramic windows. A table adorned with handwoven Wampanoag designs awaited, while the aroma of centuries-old recipes wafted in the air.

On the stove, a pot of succulent seafood stew bubbled, brimming with striped bass, bluefish, and flounder, infused with fragrant herbs from the garden. The broth sang of the ocean's embrace, and ancestral whispers drifted into the steam.

Beside the stew, bowls of "Sobaheg," the classic Wampanoag succotash, burst with extraordinary savory notes. Corn, beans, and squash, a trinity of sustenance, were harmoniously blended, each ingredient speaking of their sacred Three Sisters. The "Three Sisters" in the context of Wampanoag agriculture refers to three main crops that were traditionally grown together in a method known as companion planting. These three crops were grown in a symbiotic relationship, where each plant benefits the others, creating a balanced and sustainable agricultural system. This method of planting is not only practical but also knowledge that was specific to the tribes and shared with the pilgrims.

A modern oven, embedded seamlessly in the kitchen's rustic charm, released the scent of roasted game, venison that echoed the heartbeat of the woods, and wild turkey marinated in cranberry sauce, kissed by the tart sweetness of ancestral harvests.

In a corner, a gleaming refrigerator held berries, cherries, and apples in baskets. These fruits were ripe and were waiting to be turned into sweet handcrafted pies. Their flaky crusts a sugary continuation of culinary traditions.

The kitchen's center stage featured a stately table, adorned with traditional Wampanoag pottery, with bowls of "Nasaump," a corn pudding delicately flavored with maple syrup and berries. The bowls captured the essence of a people's connection to the land and showcased all that had been taught and learned through the centuries.

From the fridge, shelves of artisanal cranberry juice and corn beer stood as beverages of choice, while a kettle steamed with fragrant herbal tea, a brew of time-honored remedies.

As guests gathered around, the table resonated with the heartbeat of the tribe, a chorus of voices retelling tales of resilience and unity. The table was made from sturdy oak, and could easily sit twenty people. As more friends and family gathered around, Weetamoo moved to greet her weary son. She had made it a tradition to gather her tribe and introduce her hard-working handsome son every Thanksgiving as the kickoff to an entertaining holiday event. It was apparent to all that he was her rock, her pride, and her baby.

Weetamoo greeted Philip with a warm and welcoming smile. They embraced and shone like torchbearers to the tribal members who were present. The laughter of children and the cornucopia of tribal languages filled the air in tandem with the delicious smells of the Thanksgiving feast at hand. They both loved being a beacon of love and hope to the community and they were in turn appreciated by the attendees. They relaxed as they sat down to enjoy the event. The guests followed suit.

These hosted events were so popular in the community that magazine articles were written about Weetamoo's Thanksgivings. Celebrities and aristocrats made the journey just to experience her cooking. She was also a vision to behold. Weetamoo always looked in style for the event.

This Thanksgiving, Weetamoo wore a regal ribbon dress, a striking garment meticulously crafted with interesting textiles- handwoven ribbons in traditional geometric patterns. The dress was a blend of elegant modern design and cultural symbolism, with a flowing silhouette that paid homage to her ancestral roots.

Adorning her feet were beautifully beaded moccasins, where each bead was a miniature masterpiece, each one reflected the colors of the earth and sea. These moccasins were as comfortable as they were exquisite, designed for both style and comfort. Weetamoo carefully chose to wear these anytime she cooked, since she would be on her feet for hours. Draped gracefully over one of her shoulders, was a luxuriously embroidered shawl, featuring intricate beadwork and floral motifs. The shawl, though a symbol of opulence, also embodied the warmth and hospitality of the Wampanoag people.

The modern Wampanoag woman's attire was adorned with exquisite jewelry, and Weetmoo's dress was no exception. Her dress featured silver and turquoise pieces that reflected both cultural significance and contemporary sophistication

Amidst the gathering of his people, Meta, astutely rugged and timeless, stood with an aura of wisdom etched into the lines of his weathered face. He occupied the head of the table, a place of honor earned through years of reverence for tradition and guidance of his tribe.

His eyes, like deep pools of ancient knowledge, cradled the memories of generations past. His strong, calloused hands were proof of a lifetime of labor in harmony with the land, a connection that coursed through his veins.

With a voice as resonant as a mountain stream, he began a traditional Wampanoag prayer, each word a note in a sacred melody. The air hummed with the echoes of ancestors, their spirits ever-present in this moment of grace.

As the prayer concluded, the elder's hands moved with a grace that belied his years, like the gentle waves upon the shore. He carved the beautiful turkey, the centerpiece of their feast, with a precision that revealed his intimate knowledge of the land's bounty.

Onlookers, gathered in silent anticipation, gazed upon this masterful display, their hearts brimming with appreciation. They understood that the elder is not merely carving a turkey; he was carving a connection to their heritage, a reminder of their roots, and a promise of a future that honors tradition and unity. They respected Meta and his direction.

In the hushed reverence of the moment, Meta illuminated a path to Thanksgiving. One that bridged time and culture, where gratitude and tradition intermingle, and where the spirit of unity was carved into the heart of their tribe.

Cheers bellied out when finally, the turkey was ready to be shared. Bowls and plates were clanking against one another as people situated themselves for a proper acceptance of the next course being given to them. Amid the warmth and comfort of his father's Thanksgiving table, Philip's heart was a mix of relief and contentment. The gathering had a way of rekindling the embers of family ties, reminding him of the bonds he held dear.

With each bite of flounder, Philip savored not only the flavors but also the sense of belonging that enveloped him. He couldn't help but notice the sympathetic glances of aunts and uncles who, in their own way, expressed concern for his bachelorhood, their unspoken hopes that love would find him.

Yet, the moments of silent contemplation were like a guiding light, a holy breath of wisdom that encouraged him to become the best version of himself. The clinks of silverware and laughter around the table seemed to echo this call to self-improvement.

As he smiled to himself, the act of taking a forkful of flounder became a symbol of gratitude for the love that surrounded him. The gathering was a beacon of warmth, reminding Philip that his path was illuminated by the gentle embrace of family, and that romantic love, in its own time, would find its way to his heart.

Thanksgiving festivities at the Tautog's were a spirited affair that stretched into the early morning hours. As the grand feast ended, the harmony of laughter and conversation blended with the symphony of full stomachs and contented hearts.

Inside the cozy dining room, some family members and guests found themselves surrendering to the gentle pull of drowsiness. They nestled into plush armchairs, draped with cozy blankets, thanks to

Philip's sister's hospitable nature. She designed their estate to be comfortable and inviting for all. This was her time to shine. She brought around herbal tea for guests to sip on to ease their tired stomachs.

In this mosaic of moments, the Tautog family's Thanksgiving was a protective blanket woven from the threads of love, laughter, and unity. Whether napping, playing outside, or enjoying holiday melodies, the spirit of the holiday was alive in each heart, a celebration that extended into the early morning hours. Histories of past Thanksgivings illustrated unique experiences and challenges to get to this point in time. The guests knew that they relied on each other for success, and no one wanted to let anyone down.

In the tranquil glow of the living room, Meta, the elder of the Tautog family, entered regally and searched the expansive space for his son. He had just left the kitchen where robotic brooms vacuumed under the table. Any small bite of food or scrap of unfinished dessert were sucked into a robotic dustpan. Meta had invested in these along with a state-of-the-art dishwashing system to help clean up after this specific holiday.

He was glad he did as it helped his family expand the tradition. Meta scanned the room again. He finally landed on Philip, his son, who was relaxing on the sofa. Instantly, Philip's respect for his father spurred him to sit up, a gesture that spoke of the reverence he held for Meta.

Meta, his face etched with wisdom and love, placed a gentle hand on Philip's shoulder, a touch that conveyed both warmth and understanding. "Are you alright, my son?" he inquired, sensing the unspoken words that hung in the air.

In this cherished moment, father and son had the opportunity to catch up on daily affairs, to share stories and concerns that time had kept at bay. Philip's gratitude flowed from his heart, and he began to express his aspirations. "Father, I am ready," he said, his voice carrying the weight of anticipation. "I am ready to find a mate, to take the next step."

The room, now a sanctuary for the wisdom of generations, bore witness to the passage of time and the enduring strength of familial bonds. In Meta's eyes, a father's love met a son's determination, and he could not look away. He gazed into his son's beautiful brown eyes and any sense of longing or envy left his body. Meta was genuinely happy for his child, and knew that this step away from the family business would be a prosperous one. Meta secretly prayed for strength and patience as his son journeyed into the world of love for himself. Meta gave Philip his genuine blessing, and kissed Philip's hands.

As Meta responded to his son's words, his heart swelled with pride and affection. Encouragingly, he wrapped Philip in a warm and heartfelt hug, a gesture that had been somewhat embarrassing to the younger man in the past. However, this time, Philip's newfound maturity allowed him to appreciate the embrace for what it truly was – a symbol of his father's love and support.

In that embrace, Meta conveyed his unwavering pride in Philip's growth and readiness to take the next step in life. The room, filled with the legacy of their ancestors, became a sanctuary of understanding, where the passing of time only deepened the bonds of family.

Philip sat back down, looking around the room. Nothing had changed- except everything had. No one seemed to notice the exhilaration that Philip was experiencing or noted the exciting journey that lay ahead. Philip began to wonder about the beautiful woman he would share his life with. Would she have long dark hair, emerald eyes, or a sweet smile? Amidst the soft rustling of his thoughts, Philip was jolted from his daydream by the presence of an older crippled woman who approached him. Her every step spoke of a life's journey, and in that moment, he understood the importance of being polite and respectful. He realized that she was determined to speak to him and he had no idea why. With a warm and gracious smile, he extended a hand to her, a gesture of kindness and courtesy. His kingly aura left the women feeling humbled and exalted all at the same time.

The woman's voice was a delicate whisper, proof of her wisdom and experience. Philip, his tall frame hunched over her tiny form, leaned in closely to listen, a sign of his interest in her words. In the quiet exchange that followed, the passing of stories and wisdom flowed between generations, an unspoken acknowledgment of their shared cultural values.

This elder woman needed to tell him a story of his history. She began, "In the ancient woods of Patuxet, where the whispers of the wind met the murmurs of the trees, there lived a young woman, known by her people as Mahkah, a name that meant "moonlight." The year was 1616, and the land still held the fresh footprints of those who had arrived from England.

Mahkah had no ill thoughts towards these newcomers, however, her tribe was talking about them continuously. Some members of the tribe were worried that the newcomers would ruin the land or try and steal from the people. Others were intrigued at how much these foreigners seemed to know.

One evening, as the twilight painted the sky in hues of purple and gold, Mahkah ventured deeper into the forest, drawn by an unseen hand. She moved with grace, her moccasin-clad feet treading lightly upon the mossy ground. She finally arrived at a stream that cut through the sacred ground.

As she stood beneath the towering trees, their leaves a canopy of emerald and gold, a celestial being descended from the heavens. An angel, luminous and ethereal, with wings that glistened like moonbeams, appeared before Mahkah. The angel's light was reflected so brightly against the water that she could barely see.

The angel's voice was a melody, a serenade to the heart, as she spoke to Mahkah in a language that transcended words. Mahkah was guided back to her senses by the angel's voice. The angel told of a future, where unity would flourish, where the wisdom of the land and the sea would be honored, and where the tapestry of cultures would be woven into a harmonious mosaic.

In her outstretched hand, the angel held a symbolic gift, a seed that pulsed with the essence of life and growth. She planted it in the earth, and from that seed, a gigantic tree sprouted, its roots reaching deep into the land, its branches stretching to the sky. The angel plucked another seed and placed it into a necklace that was sealed shut. It was a beautiful wooden talisman that held a tiny seed in the center. The angel gently gave it to Mahkah.

Mahkah, humbled by the celestial vision before her, knew that this encounter was a sacred moment, a bridge between worlds. She understood that her people's destiny was intertwined with the promise of unity and harmony, and that this message would be passed down through generations.

The angel told Mahkah that many people on her land would die in the next three years from disease brought by the white man from the Old World. The angel told Mahkah that no matter what happened, she would be safe with the talisman and that she needed to stay calm and hopeful.

The angel also warned her that many new people would be coming to live with her and it was imperative that she stay hospitable and kind. With an unfearing heart, Mahkah accepted the wisdom and the talisman as an outward symbol of this incredible meeting. The angel promised Mahkah that her peacekeeping spirit would guide her people through many tumultuous times and that their resilience would always endure.

With a final blessing, the angel ascended to the heavens, leaving Mahkah in the quiet woods, the moonlight bathing her in a divine glow. She returned to her people with the message of the celestial being, a message of hope, unity, and the enduring legacy of the Wampanoag, a beacon that would guide her people through the ages. She cozied up near the fire where she fell into the hypnotizing blaze of the "nuppihtaquash." The older woman checked to see if Philip was still paying attention. Philip looked astounded by this story and had no words.

As the woman continued her tale, the legend unfolded, carrying the weight of wisdom and prophecy. The angel, it was said, had imparted not only a vision but also a sacred mission to Mahkah and to her descendants. It was a mission to preserve the bonds between the Wampanoag people and the newcomers, the English, who brought with them strange knowledge and a new way of life. Philip's ancestors created these alliances with the pilgrims and honored the message from the angel hoping for prosperity.

The angel's message was clear: by being kind and helpful, the tribe would create a lasting legacy. The angel advised that a member of the tribe would save an innocent woman from the tortures and hardships of her daily life and the legacy of peace world forever be perpetuated. This woman, chosen by fate, would be destined to bridge two worlds together

Through the ages, the message of the celestial being lived on, an enduring reminder of the profound importance of empathy, unity, and the preservation of peace. The Tautog family was living proof that this legend had become a reality

The woman extended a cherished artifact, the Harvest Talisman, its presence radiant with history and purpose. With a gentle and knowing smile, she spoke of its significance, of the momentous occasion it represented. She explained that, by tradition, it was her solemn duty to bestow this talisman upon Philip at the threshold of his maturity, and that this Thanksgiving marked the appointed time. It was his duty to find the women in the legend and bring forth a new generation of progress.

The Harvest Talisman, she revealed, was a symbol of protection and guidance, a shield to accompany him on the journey that lay ahead.

It was a reminder that he need not fear the path he was destined to walk, for he was surrounded by the legacy of his people and the support of those who loved him.

Confusion and hesitation mingled in Philip's eyes as he accepted the talisman, his fingers tracing the intricacies of the artifact. Its weight was both tangible and symbolic, a connection to his heritage and a promise of guidance on the road ahead.

The talisman's surface was weathered, with the wisdom of years, engraved by the hands of those who'd shed tears and blood. It showed intricate patterns of sun, moon, and sea, In the middle of it all, a simple seed laid at rest.

He felt the talisman's heartbeat, a pulse and a thrum, it encouraged the promise of home. Intrinsically linked to the spirit of the earth, A guardian and guide from the moment of birth.

With its weight in his hand, he was anchored and free, In the presence of the talisman, he found his decree. A symbol of heritage, a beacon of light, For his journey ahead, through day and through night.

With the Harvest Talisman cradled in his hand, Philip felt a newfound sense of purpose and wonder about the path that lay before him. He turned to the woman, gratitude shining in his eyes, and said, "Thank you," from the depths of his heart.

As he left the gathering for his own home, he set forth into the night, the Harvest Talisman a steadfast companion, Philip embraced the future with a spirit of gratitude, anticipation, and the knowledge that his destiny was woven by his people's legacy.

In that moment, as Philip walked past the fountain in front of his family's estate, the Harvest Talisman in hand, an inexplicable burning sensation surged through his palm, sending tingles coursing through his veins. He watched in awe as a magnetic pull, a mysterious force, drew streams of water from the fountain to cascade around him, a swirling dance of liquid and light.

Enveloped in a soft, ethereal glow, he felt weightless, as if the very laws of gravity and time had been suspended. The world around him blurred, and he was thrust upward, as if being carried by a funnel composed of the absence of matter and the embrace of cosmic forces.

Amidst the swirling maelstrom, he clung to the promise he had made to be brave, and the quest to find true love that had beckoned him. This created a positive energy flow and the power of his focused thoughts and intentions guided him into a nebula. The nebula gently released him, and in that moment, the familiar grounds of his family's estate dissolved into a muddy stream, and he found himself transported to a place where the boundaries of reality blurred, and the adventure of a lifetime began.

As Philip lay in the muddy embrace of his newfound surroundings, he felt like a fish out of water. The normal buzz of daily life had vanished, replaced by a profound silence that enveloped him. Time seemed elusive, and he struggled to recognize the season, though the chill in the air hinted at a late night.

He observed the gentle shimmer of moonlight on the nearby stream, its waters reflecting the mystery of this place. The earth beneath him was moist and marked by the recent rain, a reminder of nature's ever-turning cycles.

Though confusion initially clouded his thoughts, Philip's mind began to untangle itself, like a delicate web weaving its threads back together. In the stillness, he was grateful there were no large bears or predators nearby. The solitude, while disorienting, allowed him to gather his thoughts and contemplate the journey that lay ahead.

With determination coursing through his veins, Philip rose from the muddy ground, the Harvest Talisman still clutched tightly in his hand. His clothes, however, provided evidence of a harrowing journey-His clothes were scared and tattered from traveling inside a black hole, reconvening within a nebula, and finally, being spewed out of the tail end of a tornado. He was grateful that only his clothes had been ripped and torn by the inexplicable passage through time and space.

The primal instinct for survival surged within him, a visceral force that transcended all that he had known about the world. It was as if this new world had stripped away the layers of familiarity and revealed the raw of existence.

In this moment of profound transformation, Philip felt a surge of vitality and resilience. His senses sharpened, and he knew that he needed to navigate this unfamiliar terrain, to adapt and overcome. The beliefs and certainties of his former life were no longer relevant; he was now an imposter in the same region he had grown and thrived in.

He walked for hours, traversing the terrain with a spirit of humility and curiosity, aware that this world was both a mystery and an opportunity. His footsteps were imprints of goodwill, and his voice, a bridge to connection.

In 1616, this Wampanoag village stood, where nature and spirit entwined, A timeless quilt of heritage, in the heart and soul of humankind. With reverence for the land and sea, their legacy forever sung, in this sanctuary of the past, where the ancient and the present were one.

The village was nestled beside the forest. The people were also thriving, their spirits alive, in this tranquil, timeless space. Within the lodge, fires burned bright, casting warm and flickering light, as stories and songs filled the air.

Cornfields stretched, a sea of green, in the season of life's rebirth. Vibrant gardens of herbs and squash, tended by hands that knew their worth. Elders spoke of traditions, the teachings of ancestors held dear, while children danced with laughter, with dreams of the future clear.

The earthy scent of cedar and pine, a fragrant embrace on the breeze, led Philip to the fire inside the village. The village, a cluster of wigwams, their silhouettes rising tall and strong, embraced the heartbeat of the land, where ancient stories were passed along and speculation about the future were revealed. Philip knew he had to be careful to approach these people in their home. He was a stranger, and he knew all too well how this interaction could end.

Around a crackling fire, a tribe huddled together on a chilly night, their faces kissed by the flickering flames, their spirits seeking warmth and light. A pall of weariness hung in the air, like a shroud of fog and haze, As the people sought solace in the fire's embrace, in this peaceful, tranquil daze.

They sat in silence, wrapped in blankets, the tribe of aching bones, Aches and sniffles, and somber sighs, their weariness plainly shown. Yet amidst the gathering, a young girl sat, untouched by autumn's sting.

In her hands, she cradled a basket of cracked corn, its earthy scent a cure, as she nibbled on the kernels, her heart so light and pure. Her eyes, a beacon of health and hope, shone with youthful grace. The young girl's laughter broke the stillness, a melody soft and sweet, A reminder of the strength of kinship, the circle of life complete.

As the leader of the tribe, a figure of wisdom and warmth, observed Philip's approach, he sensed the essence of a kindred spirit, and his worries melted away. The tribe, with their relaxed and open demeanor, had a long-standing tradition of welcoming visitors.

With a serene smile, the leader stepped forward to greet Philip, extending a hand in friendship. "Greetings, traveler," he said with a voice like the gentle flow of a river, "I am Tawodi, the leader of our tribe. Welcome to our village."

Tawodi's presence exuded a quiet authority, his eyes revealing a depth of knowledge and experience that had been nurtured by the land

and the people he had led. In his welcoming gesture, Philip felt the bonds of hospitality and a sense of belonging, as if he had found a sanctuary in the heart of the tribe.

The bonds of friendship formed swiftly, and Philip's genuine and humble nature had endeared him to the tribe. In a warm display of hospitality, he was offered a bed in the lodge, the heart of their community, in exchange for his assistance with the harvest the following day. He accepted and began his trek to the lodge. The young girl noticed his talisman and gave him a soft and knowing smile. He could tell she recognized it, but he was quickly swept away to his new housing.

As he lay on the cot within the welcoming embrace of the lodge, the flickering firelight danced across the wooden beams. He thought of the knowing look in the girl's eyes as she saw the talisman dangling from his neck. *Had she brought him here?* He wondered. The day's journey had tired him out, and the questions about the reality of his newfound experiences gradually faded into the background as his chilly body finally surrendered to sleep.

The morning sun filtered through the woven walls of Philip's room, casting a warm, dappled light that gently roused him from slumber. As he blinked away the remnants of sleep, a pair of energetic young men entered his space. Their eyes sparkled with curiosity as they surveyed the newcomer, sensing that there was something interesting about this visitor.

With spirited gestures and warm smiles, they reached out to Philip and extended an invitation to join them outside. Eager to explore and connect with the tribe further, Philip followed them into the morning air, where the scents of cooking breakfast wafted through the camp. His mouth was dry and he could tell there was no toothpaste around. He knew his hair was a tangled mess, and his clothes were almost obsolete

Around a crackling fire, two burly, surly women were tending to a bubbling pot, their laughter ringing through the air as they worked their fare. The aroma of food being prepared over an open flame filled the senses, a warm and inviting symphony of flavors. It reminded Philip of his own mother. He knew he could not be seen as absentminded, so he quickly changed his mind and approached the women thoughtfully.

The women cast a welcoming glance toward Philip. With an understanding born of the heart, they recognized a kindred spirit in this visitor, someone who had to become a part of their daily rhythm, their community, and their shared moments around the fire.

The women reached out to him and encouraged him to eat breakfast. Their hospitality and interest grounded Philip. He looked at them with a pitiful gaze. Instead of meeting it, the women looked at him in awe and wonder. With a sense of rebirth and a newfound identity, Philip introduced himself as Tautog, a name that carried future promise.

His decision to adopt this new identity gave the tribe pause, and some wondered if he might be a wanderer who had strayed from a neighboring tribe. They inquired if he wished to stay among them, understanding that sometimes life's path led people in unexpected directions. He plead with them that he would in fact like to stay. Without judgement, he and the tribe ate their bountiful breakfast-squash stew. He enjoyed it, even thought it was not like his mother's.

Tautog found himself embraced not only by their knowledge and traditions but also by their nurturing spirit. The tribe recognized the importance of hygiene for one's well-being and showed him their ways of staying clean and healthy.

Each morning, the tribe would gather by the sparkling stream, where the waters ran clear jond pure. They would show Tautog how to use natural materials and plants, like fragrant cedar leaves and sweetgrass, to create herbal infusions and soaps that left the skin refreshed and revitalized. It was a lesson in harmony with the land and a deep respect for the environment.

As Tautog adopted these practices, he found himself not only feeling cleaner but also more connected to the rhythms of the natural world. He found himself looking forward to the chilly immersion therapy daily. As soon as he was clean, he would hop out and head over to the campfire where he would use his fingers to detangle his growing mane. The tribe's wisdom became a part of his daily routine, a bridge to a deeper understanding of the land and its gifts.

Clothing was another vital aspect of hygiene and protection from the elements. The tribe, recognizing Tautog's need, provided him with garments woven from the fibers of native plants like milkweed and yucca, as well as the supple hides of animals they had hunted. These clothing items were practical, comfortable, and allowed for flexibility in movement, essential for a life closely intertwined with nature. The tribe even gifted him his own beautiful moccasinash.

Tautog's appreciation for the tribe's teachings and their generosity in sharing their ways of life extended beyond hygiene and clothing. It inspired his own generosity and openness. His resourcefulness and knowledge were evident, and the tribe saw in him the potential to be a valuable member of their community. Recognizing his willingness to contribute, they assigned him a role as a fisherman, a task that would not only provide sustenance for the tribe but also allow Tautog to forge deeper connections and build a new life in this place of warmth and acceptance.

Tautog's presence stirred a growing interest within the tribe, his daily interactions becoming a bridge between two worlds. He approached each day with a vow to share his knowledge, offering glimpses of the world beyond while also learning from the tribe's traditions and way of life. His past life had adequately prepared for the envy and jealousy he encountered and helped him overcome these obstacles to teach and guide the tribe.

As Tautog became a respected member of the Wampanoag tribe, he recognized an opportunity to share his knowledge of modern and sustainable fishing methods. With an appreciation for the environment and a commitment to preserving their natural resources, the tribe eagerly embraced his teachings.

Tautog gathered the interested members of the tribe by the waterside, a place where they had fished for generations. He began by explaining the importance of sustainable fishing, ensuring that they caught enough to sustain the community without harming the delicate balance of the eco-system.

He introduced modern fishing techniques, such as catch and release, and showed them how to make and use eco-friendly fishing gear. This gear included: Fishing nets- nets made from plant fibers such as jute, hemp, or flax were commonly used. These fibers were biodegradable and sustainable. Fishermen would fashion these fibers into a net design that allowed fish to be caught without harming the fish population. The size of the mesh was often designed to allow smaller, juvenile fish to escape, ensuring the sustainability of the fishery. Fishing hooks- hooks were crafted from natural materials such as wood, bone, or even thorns. These materials were biodegradable and would break down over time if lost in the water. By using barbless hooks, fishermen could minimize harm to fish, making it easier to release undersized or unwanted catches. Bait- sustainable bait options included insects, grubs, or natural plant-based baits. Fishermen would forage for bait in their local environment, ensuring minimal disruption to the eco-system. Fishing lines- fishing lines were often made from natural materials like plant fibers or animal sinews. These materials were strong and resilient, making them suitable for use in fishing. They would naturally decompose over time. Traps and weirs- fish traps and weirs were constructed using local, biodegradable materials like sticks, reeds, and rocks.

These allowed for the capture of fish in a way that was both effective and sustainable. Beyond gear, responsible fishing practices were also essential. These practices included adhering to seasonal fishing regulations, respecting fish spawning areas, and observing catch limits.

Tautog emphasized the importance of understanding the local fish species and their habitats. He also taught them how to read the signs of the environment, like changes in water temperature and the behavior of aquatic life, to improve their fishing success.

The tribe members listened attentively and observed Tautog's demonstrations, eager to embrace these sustainable practices. They asked questions and sought to fully understand the principles of responsible fishing.

With newfound knowledge and determination, the tribe members set out on their first fishing expedition using these sustainable methods. They worked together, mindful of the delicate balance of nature, and caught enough fish to feed the community without depleting the local fish populations.

The tribe welcomed his teachings with open hearts, and while Tautog's memories of history were not as vivid as he wished, he shared what he could, connecting the dots of the past and the present. The gentle exchange of knowledge and wisdom became a cornerstone of their unity and respect for one another.

One day, he noticed the young woman he saw the first day he had arrived. She smiled warmly at him. He felt peace but did not feel passionately towards her. His mind began to drift and he wondered if this was indeed the woman from the legend. The local fishermen broke his thoughts by yelling his name and requesting that he check their nets. He welcomed the distraction and got back to work, chewing on mint as he went.

Tautog's journey had transformed him in ways he never could have foreseen. He never felt braver than he did in these moments of sharing, for he had been gifted with wisdom from the centuries and the profound responsibility of passing it on to his newfound community.

Each day held the promise of new beginnings, fresh insights, and the beauty of learning and teaching in unison.

As he stood before the tribe, his heart brimming with the weight and grace of history, Tautog understood that his path had led him to a place of significance. With each lesson, he wove the threads of time together into a mutual understanding, and the tribe, in turn, gifted him with the warmth of their acceptance and their own stories.

In this union of past and present, Tautog embraced his role as a guardian of knowledge and a beacon of hope for the future. The days unfolded like pages of a never-ending story, where the wisdom of the ages became a guiding light, leading the tribe forward into the uncharted territory of tomorrow. The only exception was that Philip knew the truth. He knew how disease killed almost all of the people he was surrounded by in the next three years. This truth nagged at his heart daily as he fought to create a cleaner and safer place for his new family.

At night, he would lie awake thinking of the luxuries of his old life. He missed his family and the ability to communicate quickly and easily. He pushed these feelings down with gratitude and his thoughts always circled back to how he could use his experiences from the future to reshape his present circumstances. Silently, he fell into a deep sleep.

Chapter Two- Colonizing Patuxet

THE CHIEF OF THE HERRING Pond area tribe, Tawodi, and Tautog became almost inseparable. Tautog had been with the tribe for almost six months when he had his first custom deerskin breachcloth and leggings made for him by the women in the tribe. Feather, to be exact.

Feather was a beautiful young woman in the tribe. She always painted her face with beautiful red and white Feathers. Her hair was soft and flowy and she wore feather armbands. She was the niece of Massasoit, and Tautog knew she was off limits.

When the tribe did their annual Herring runs, Tautog was known to strip down to just his deerskin, so as not to get bogged down by any excess. Tawodi made sure that Tautog had his face painted with red or yellow ocher, black from charcoal and graphite, or white from clay with images of fish swimming on his body.

When Tawodi and Toutog were out fishing one day, they ran across a group of European men bathing by the river. Toutog knew to stay away from them simply because he knew not to hunt where people were bathing and using the bathroom. He directed Tawodi to go further upstream. The pair did so, and experienced a great day's catch.

Taking it back to camp that evening, Tawodi told Toutog how proud he was of him. "I am so glad you decided to join our tribe and stay. I know it has not been easy for you." Toutog lit up like a campfire himself. He was not used to hearing words of praise, and it made him happier than a clam. "Thank you, Chief. That means a lot coming from you." Toutog was thrilled he had the chance to earn a position in his new community.

The women in the tribe saw Toutog as a smart and energetic bachelor. They would gossip about him when he was not around. Some of the more eligible ladies even speculated on why he was single and how someone could let him go. Toutog despised the attention, and he made a mental note to stay far away from the women when he did not need them.

Toutog was open to the idea of love. He loved walking through the ladies as they were getting ready for the day. He loved eating their meals and listening to them sing to the children. He enjoyed providing for them, and saw the possibility of marrying one of them. *Would that make the legend come true?* He asked himself almost daily. How would he know if he had fulfilled his duty? Would there be any signs? He replayed what the old woman was telling him over and over in his mind. He had accepted the Harvest Talisman and in doing so, also accepted that his instincts would lead him to the woman he was supposed to save. He left it up to the Heavens to led the way.

He did not have a lot of time to think it through because soon an epidemic was hitting the people of his tribe. It wasn't only his tribe that was suffering. Word spread faster than the disease, and it appeared that smallpox, influenza, and other viruses were spreading to the Native Americans who did not have any immunity built up. The Europeans had contaminated the land and animals, and nature had turned against the beloved Native people. Tautog found himself nourishing the warriors, laborers, and teachers with his fish, but he could not keep up.

Members of the tribe, once sniffling around the campfire, were falling over dead, coughing up blood, or dying in their sleep on a regular basis. Work around the camp and in the fields went undone, and it was not a surprising scene to see children eating crops directly from the field to feed their bellies as the rest of the crop was left to be destroyed from lack of tending. On one Spring day, Toutog counted as many as 260 tribal members dead. He took leave from his post as fisherman to help dig a mass grave for his family members.

A great sadness descended upon the Herring Pond tribe, enveloping them in a heavy shroud of grief and despair. It was a scene of heart-wrenching sorrow, as the impact of diseases brought by European settlers took its toll on the Indigenous community. It was all Tautog could do to not let his heart be filled with resentment and bitterness. He had a habit of tending to his thoughts, but he knew others in the tribe were not as knowledgeable or disciplined. If only he had the silver bullet that could end the isolation, sickness, and sadness that marred his people.

Within the village, once alive with the interesting sounds of laughter and communal gatherings, there was now a haunting silence. The air was heavy with the scent of burning sage and sweetgrass, an outward symbol of the tribe's prayers for healing and protection.

Families huddled together, their faces etched with worry and fear. Elders, the bearers of ancient wisdom, lay frail and weakened, their stories and teachings threatened to be lost forever. The sound of ceremonial drums had grown quiet, replaced by the somber rhythm of mourning.

The community's strength had been tested, and the loss of loved ones was felt deeply. Nine out of ten tribal members were killed during the course of three years leading up to 1620 from these communal diseases. The faces of those who remained were marked by both resilience and a profound sense of grief. They mourned the loss of their ancestors, children, and friends, all victims of illnesses brought by newcomers who had sought to settle the land.

The European settlers were few and far between. Many had died of harsh conditions or simply gave up. The survivors during this time were looking for ways to bond and grow together without causing more suffering. Tautog realized their frustration and confusion during this time. The people did not have a clear understanding as to why this was happening or how to stop it.

The tribe used medicinal plants to mitigate the diseases and cope with recovery. They had ceremonies that helped the community heal from their grief. They moved away from contaminated areas and limited their interactions with settlers, and isolated from each other. It was a dark time, but the People of the First Light refused to give up.

It was a time of profound sorrow, but even in the midst of their pain, the Herring Pond tribe found solace in the bonds of their community. They comforted one another, holding onto the hope that their traditions, culture, and spirit would endure, and that they would find a way to heal and rebuild, preserving their legacy. The community shrank significantly in size, and those who were able carried the burden of raising the children and gathering resources to help the tribe prosper.

The once jovial and welcoming tribe had become hollowed and heavyhearted. The yoke was heavy and the people felt the weight of the world on their shoulders. It is no wonder that they were collectively weary when they saw the Mayflower reach the port in Cape Cod on November 11, 1620.

The year of our Lord, 1605 brought many changes to John Alden. He was a middle-aged man with a beautiful wife named Sarah. They had dated and married in Scrooby. It was a quaint town, and John and Sarah had a humble marriage. Their parents were neighbors and they grew up going to the same school. The Church of England was prospering and Sarah's family was coping with the change. Historically, Sarah's ancestors were raised Roman Catholic.

John noticed how difficult it was for Sarah to suffer through being mandated to go to a Church she did not agree with. Years of torture built up inside of her. She found herself learning Latin and going to Catholic Mass underground. She dodged prison, but John was not so lucky.

On their wedding day, the religious climate had shifted. Sarah and John were married on a beautiful Spring day in Scrooby. The ceremony was based on the Book of Common Prayer, which provided a structured liturgy. The ceremony included prayers, readings from the Bible, and the exchange of vows. The priest officiated the wedding, and the couple made solemn promises to each other. Sarah was depressed the entire time because she was not able to have her marriage sanctified by a Catholic priest.

They exchanged small metal wedding bands during their nuptial mass. The couple excitedly left the Church, and their families threw rice at them. Sarah had complained about it getting in her hair, and she and John laughed about it on the way to their celebratory feast. That was the best day of John's life. Sarah and John danced the night away, and they soon became inseparable. John recognized and felt sorry for Sarah's plight. His protective instinct grew along with his intolerance for the oppression and persecution his wife faced daily for her faith.

John was a Separatist. He hated knowing there was no separation between Church and State. He hated being persecuted by Church officials. He was always being fined and sent to prison for his nonconforming attitude and belief that he was free to believe the way he wanted. John had been sent to prison for not attending the Church of England Services and for going to religious meetings outside of the Church. Prison was a lonely place for John. He was stuck in a dimly lit cell on a straw mattress. He barely ate and was always cold. It reminded him of when Paul was imprisoned. All he wanted to do was pray the entire day. When he was released, he was expected to conform to the standards of the day and deal with his wife.

This was not an arrangement that would work in John's favor, and he perceived it as persecution for his beliefs. He not only wanted to purify the Church, he wanted clear distinctions between the government and the Church. Mainly, he wanted Sarah to be happy.

Eventually, Sarah grew faint from the stress and fell ill. She was taken to the hospital to deliver her baby. The dimly lit room of the 17th-century English hospital was filled with hushed whispers, the muted sounds of suffering, and the faint glow of candles that flickered against the cold stone walls. The air was heavy with the scent of herbs and tinctures used in medical treatments of the time. In one corner of the room, a woman lay on a narrow, uncomfortable bed, her husband kneeling beside her in prayer. Sarah was not allowed to receive the Anointing of the Sick blessing by a priest. John secretly practiced the ritual and performed it on his wife.

"Oh, Lord, have mercy upon me. Please, protect this child." Sarah gasped for air.

Sarah's face was contorted with pain, and her hands clenched the sheets as she struggled through the agonizing ordeal of childbirth. The nurses, clad in simple, rough-spun garments, moved hurriedly around her, doing their best to provide comfort and assistance.

"Breathe, my dear. Breathe. It'll be over soon." The nurse said softly.

Despite their efforts, it was evident that Sarah's condition was deteriorating rapidly. The midwife, an experienced but weathered woman, did her best to help guide the difficult delivery. As the moments passed, it became clear that the situation was dire. The midwife did everything in her power, but in the end, the struggle was too much. Sarah's gasps grew weaker, and with a final, desperate push, she brought a fragile life into the world even as her own was slipping away. The room fell into a mournful silence as the woman took her last breath. The nurses gently placed the newborn, a tiny, crying bundle, into a nearby cradle. John, his face wet with tears, grieved the loss of his beloved wife. The cries of the newborn filled the room, a bittersweet reminder of the precious and fragile nature of life.

Days turned into weeks and John could barely get up the desire and energy to go to work. He was a therapist by trade, and even he needed one now. John was convinced the treatment Sarah received was the cause of her death. He officially hated England.

He and his family members planned on going to the Netherlands where they would be free from religious persecution. It took him two years to make the move. His daughter, Silvia, was just walking when they arrived in their new home. In the heart of the bustling Dutch town, young Silvia found her feet, not on English soil but on the cobblestone streets of Leiden. She was but a tender toddler, her eyes wide with wonder, and her heart was full of the promise of a new life, a life free from the religious persecution that had driven her family from their homeland. Hand in hand with her doting father, they embarked on a beautiful journey, and together, they danced the dance of first steps.

Silvia thrived in their new environment and loved going to school with the Dutch. Silvia was not merely learning the Dutch language; she was learning to understand the Dutch way of life, their traditions, and their kindness. She was becoming a part of her new community, her heart now bound to both her English roots and her Dutch home.

As Silvia's wooden shoes traversed the cobbled streets, she knew that she was no longer an outsider. The Dutch people had not only welcomed her but embraced her with open hearts, and in turn, Silvia had begun to assimilate not just into a new culture but into a family of diverse people. John noticed that the people would leave him alone and would dote on Silvia. The therapist inside him hated that other people were raising his daughter and shaping her life. He knew that they were doing it to save their own culture.

John loved the religious tolerance and he also loved living in a European powerhouse for culture, science, and economic prosperity.

He would lavish praise on Silvia and pray for her nightly. At night, when everything was still, John would lay awake thinking of Sarah. He saw her in Silvia, and he desperately wished he could share this journey with her physically. Sadness passed away to acceptance each and every night. In the morning, John would wake up and make the best of his day. John felt that he was fighting an uphill battle as he struggled to pay bills and raise his beautiful daughter.

The entire congregation that John had traveled with had close ties and stuck together. They formed babysitting pods, shared resources, and prayed together. When Silvia was 12, it was obvious that the Dutch wanted John and his congregation to assimilate into the Dutch way of life. They encouraged the Pilgrim's children to join the Dutch military and the Pilgrim's worried that the Dutch would eradicate their children and their religious heritage if they did not comply.

John Alden still had a lot of fight left in him. He was not going to take this lying down. He was committed to providing the best life for his daughter. He and a hundred other Pilgrim's planned to travel to the New World. He knew he could not escape reality; however, he could change it!

A few months after this revelation, John got word from a fellow European, Matt Brewster, that his congregation could sail on their mercantile ships, the Speedwell and the Mayflower to New England. All Brewster requested is that the group work hard in the New World and pay them back for the voyage. John thought this was an extreme version of an adventure. Brewster quelled his fears by providing evidence that Europeans had already been in the New World for over a hundred years. He made it sound enticing and vital to the mission of living a free life.

John stayed up late one evening, and headed over to the local tavern. There was a lot of commotion, and that drew him in. In the dimly lit, cozy interior of a 17th-century Dutch tavern, the air was thick with the warmth of camaraderie and the rich scent of ale. Patrons clinked tankards and laughed, and the flickering candles cast an amber glow upon the oak tables and the rough-hewn beams overhead. Amid this rustic merriment stood a distinguished man, impeccably dressed in the fashion of the era, his attire exuding wealth and refinement.

John approached the man, and asked about the New World. The investor opened up a leather satchel and pulled out a watercolor painting of crops and lush green spaces. John was instantly interested. The investor went on to say that illnesses had killed off many Native Americans, and the ones who were left were interested in trade. The investor asked if John had heard about Jamestown. "You simply must go!" he said convincingly. John agreed, and the next day he agreed to Brewster's terms.

The rustic Dutch tavern had slowly begun to empty as the night grew older, with patrons dispersing to their homes, leaving a tranquil hush in its wake. John Alden, having indulged in conversation and a tankard of ale, knew it was time to return home. The streets glistened with the reflection of the moon, and the chilly night air brought a comforting sense of clarity.

With each step, John felt a sense of purpose guiding him back to his cherished family. The distant sound of a hooting owl in a nearby tree seemed to serenade his path, echoing the tranquility of the hour. In his pocket, he carried the paper of the watercolor painting.

Upon returning to their modest but cozy Dutch home, John entered with silent footsteps, not wanting to disturb the peaceful slumber of his beloved Silvia. There, on the small cot beside the hearth, lay Silvia, her chest gently rising and falling with each tranquil breath. Moonlight streamed in through the leaded glass window, casting soft silvery highlights upon her sleeping form.

With great care, John began to prepare breakfast, savoring the act of preparing a morning meal for his family. The scent of bread toasting over the open fire mingled with the aroma of fresh eggs, and the gentle hiss of a pot of boiling water was like a whispered promise of what the day would hold.

As the morning sun began to cast a warm glow through the window, Silvia's eyelashes fluttered, and she awoke. Her eyes, a reflection of the morning sky, met John's with affectionate curiosity. John sat beside her, a look of tenderness in his gaze as he cradled her hand.

"Silvia," he began, his voice soft and full of anticipation, "I have some news. There is a new opportunity for us, a better place where we can make a fresh start, find new joys, and build our future together."

Silvia's eyes sparkled with a mixture of surprise and excitement, her heart stirred by John's unwavering love and their shared journey through life's adventures. She knew that wherever they were headed, they would face it together, hand in hand, just as they always had.

She already knew she had to tell her Dutch friends goodbye. In the following weeks, she broke the news to her friends. They were excited for her and sad to lose her all at the same time. She wrote down their addresses so she could write to them in the future.

The weeks that followed were all about preparation. John helped get the necessities for their voyage along with other Separatists. They had a shared mission and vision, and they could not wait to make it a reality. They finally had a scheduled date at the Plymouth port to board the Mayflower. It took months of planning and hard work, but the Pilgrims were finally on their way to unlimited potential in the New World.

The desire to start a separate colony of their own and to live in connection to God and man in a righteous way appealed so heavily to the Pilgrims, that 102 men and women embarked on a dangerous 66-day trip to New England in the bottom of a mercantile ship used for carrying cargo. The Pilgrim's knew the trip they were about to embark on was dangerous and that they would not be returning to Crown and Country ever again. After some reflection, John felt more like a fatalist than a Separatist. He did not let the notion seep into his mind, and he boarded the boat.

John knew that the path to freedom was going to be a rocky one. Not only did they have to fend off the Native Americans, they would also have to fight for their freedom from British influence and rule. Alden understood the power and control King James wanted to hold over his family, and he relished the thought of being able to walk away from that religiously oppressive ruler with confidence. His confidence rested in God, and Jesus was his rock. He could not fail.

They faced many challenges at sea. John journaled every night about the type of government and colony he would create with his fellow man. At night, they would discuss rules and law around barrels of rum and bags of tobacco. The voyage turned treacherous. The Speedwell had to turn back because of leaks, separating entire family units

As the Mayflower sailed across the vast and treacherous expanse of the Atlantic, the journey that would forever be etched in the annals of history took an unexpected turn. The fickle mistress of the seas, unforgiving and unpredictable, had a new challenge in store for the brave souls aboard.

Nights descended upon the Mayflower, the sky was shrouded in darkness. The only guidance came from the shimmering stars overhead, and the seasoned sailors worked tirelessly to keep the ship on course. Their eyes, weary from days of vigilance, scanned the horizon for any signs of danger.

It was on one fateful night that the lookout spotted ominous sails on the distant horizon. Panic spread through the ship as the realization dawned upon the passengers: pirates were on the prowl. The crew sprang into action, battening down hatches and preparing to defend their precious cargo.

The perilous passage across the Atlantic had become even more harrowing, but their resolve had not wavered. The Mayflower continued its journey, carrying the hopes and dreams of a new beginning to the shores of an unknown land. The passengers had faced not only the unforgiving sea but also the specter of piracy. Yet, their determination to reach a better future was unshakable, and they would face whatever challenges lay ahead.

The Mayflower had safely anchored in the waters off the coast of the New World in December, but the challenges that lay ahead were far from over. The unforgiving winter of 1620 brought with its harsh conditions that would test the Pilgrims' determination and resilience. As the Mayflower lay anchored off the coast, the passengers and crew disembarked onto the unfamiliar shores of Cape Cod. The crisp December air stung their cheeks, and they were met with the desolate and barren landscape that would be their new home. It was nothing like the picture John Alden had been given. John held up the bountiful watercolor painting of lush hills and compared it to the white flat shore he was looking at. He could not help but feel resolute in spite of his disappointment.

The first winter in the New World proved to be brutal, with cold and damp conditions taking their toll on the weary travelers. Sickness and disease ran rampant through their ranks, and many fell ill. The harsh winter winds and biting cold were unrelenting, bringing suffering and despair to those who had sought a better life. The death toll steadily rose as the Pilgrims struggled to cope with the harsh conditions. The graves of the fallen marked the landscape, stark reminders of the price they paid for their journey. The survivors, grieving and weakened, resolved to carry on and build a better future in this untamed land. They felt a welcoming peace and understanding that they could not comprehend.

In the depths of winter, the Pilgrims, clad in heavy coats and scarves, embarked on a series of journeys to the nearby shores. Ten rowboats would head to shore any given morning. The men, women, and children rowed through icy waters, their boats laden with supplies and tools to build their fledgling colony. The journey was perilous, and each stroke of the oars carried them closer to their destiny. The only respite from the devastations the Alden's were experiencing, was the daily boating outings Silvia would take with John to their new colonial land.

One fine day, Silvia was rowing with her dad and he told her, "No salt now, alright?" Silvia agreed. The fresh air entered her lungs and the relief and freedom she felt was almost unfathomable. Silvia had to be the richest, freest. and morally wealthiest person the world had ever encountered. Her diet had been rich in salt during her journey, and now she wanted to release it all. John sat back on the boat and grinned knowing that the excursion had been worth it.

Upon reaching the shore, the Pilgrims began their laborious task of building shelters and establishing their colony. The cold, hardened ground and their aching bodies were no match for their unwavering determination. They set to work with resolve, creating the foundation for a new life in the New World. Each day, Silvia would gather rocks and wood while her father bartered and built their very own cabin. At the end of each day, they would head back to the ship, where they were not able to even stand up straight, due to the low ceilings. S

The Alden's lived on the Mayflower for four months over the winter. The first step in building Plymouth involved clearing the land. Men and women, dressed in sturdy work attire, used axes and saws to fell trees and clear the dense forests that surrounded the area. The sound of wood being cut and the earthy scent of freshly exposed soil filled the air. Once the land was cleared, the settlers began to lay the foundations for their dwellings. They marked the boundaries of their future homes and cabins, using ropes and simple surveying tools. Wooden stakes were driven into the ground to outline where the walls of their structures would stand.

Log cabins, made from felled trees, were the primary form of housing in Plymouth. Men and women worked together to haul heavy logs, skillfully stacking them to form the walls of their cabins. Mud and straw were used to seal gaps between the logs, providing insulation and protection from the elements.

The construction of the colony's cabins was not limited to walls. Thatched roofs, made from local materials such as reeds and grasses, were carefully layered and secured to create durable and weather-resistant coverings. The thatching process required precision and teamwork.

Beyond the cabins, other structures took shape. A communal meetinghouse, a kitchen, a fort for protection, and various outbuildings began to dot the landscape. Each structure served a specific purpose in the growing community, and the settlers worked diligently to ensure their completion.

Roads and pathways were cleared to connect the various parts of the colony. These trails allowed for the efficient movement of people, goods, and livestock. Stones and gravel were used to create walkways that could withstand the New England weather.

The physical act of building Plymouth was a collaborative and labor-intensive process. The settlers' hands were marked by the toil of hard work, and their collective efforts transformed a wild and untamed land into a thriving community. Plymouth Colony was proof to the fact that Pilgrims' determination, resourcefulness, and the unity made their dreams of freedom and self-governance a reality.

When they finally rowed their boat into port for the last time, John and Silvia knew they were going to their own log cabin that John had built with his fellow Pilgrim's. The log cabin was a modest yet comfortable abode, filled with the warmth of a roaring hearth. The cabin's interior was adorned with handmade furniture, crafted with care by John himself. A wooden table stood in the center, surrounded by rough-hewn chairs, a testament to the Pilgrims' resourcefulness.

John and Silvia began the process of unpacking their belongings. Boxes and trunks held their meager possessions, cherished reminders of their former life in England. The soft glow of candlelight illuminated the room as they carefully arranged their few belongings on the wooden shelves.

Silvia moved with a wisdom beyond her fifteen years as she beamed with happiness as she moved about the cabin's small but efficient kitchen. In a black cauldron suspended over the hearth, she prepared a hearty meal for her father. The fragrant aroma of stew filled the cabin, carrying with it a sense of comfort and belonging.

As John and Silvia sat down at their wooden table, the cauldron of stew took center stage. The family shared not only a meal but also their hopes, dreams, and a sense of unity in their new life.

The first spoonful of stew was a revelation—a comforting blend of flavors that warmed their bodies and souls. The tender venison, the earthy vegetables, and the rich broth provided sustenance and a connection to the land they were learning to call home. John finally began to let his walls down, but he noticed that Silvia needed a bit more discipline.

How do you discipline a child who was able to build an entire community and skilled in the art of home-making. John couldn't help but feel a swell of pride rise within him. He instantly felt remorse and tried to understand how God wanted him to lead his family.

He longed for Sarah to be here to witness this occasion. He had a pendant with her photo in it, and he would look at it often while he built their home. Silvia was becoming a young woman and it would be helpful to have other women around. Only 52 people survived the winter and Spring, so there were not many people he could turn to. He knew his community needed to do serious outreach if they wanted to survive.

He spent the rest of the evening enjoying his daughter's company. She sat down quietly to needlepoint while he prepared his therapy business for a fresh start. Now that John was free, he was able to breath new creativity into his business.

John was a true pioneer into modern day psychology. He did not know it at the time. He believed that every person deserved dignity, and he was diligent in his pursuit of fairness and equality for everyone.

In the 1600s, mental health issues were often viewed through a religious and spiritual lens. People believed that psychological distress could be caused by sins, possession by evil spirits, or divine punishment. As a result, those seeking therapy or guidance often turned to religious figures such as priests or ministers.

One common therapeutic practice involved the process of confession and repentance. Individuals would confide in a religious authority about their struggles, sins, or emotional distress. The clergy would then offer spiritual guidance, prescribe prayers, and suggest acts of penance as a means of seeking forgiveness and relief from mental anguish.

In addition to spiritual guidance, some people sought help from healers who used herbal remedies and natural therapies. These practitioners might have offered herbal potions, tinctures, or poultices to alleviate physical and emotional symptoms. These remedies were based on traditional knowledge of plants and their medicinal properties.

Silvia Alden may be young, but she was determined to help her father's business. She knew all about baking and cooking, and the healing power of nourishment. She made a mental note while stitching to learn as much as she could about the herbs and foods surrounding her new home. *This is going to be huge!* She thought to herself. Her Dutch friends would hardly believe what she was about to discover.

Beneath the thatched roof, in the hush of the night, Silvia, in slumber, embraced dreams' soft light. Her eyes gently closed, to the land of the dream, As stars overhead in the night's quiet gleam. She did not know how special she was or how high her dreams would grow. She did not put limits on herself, and in her fantasies God's plan would begin to show.

In her cabin, cozy, with love all around, her dreams took her to places uncharted, unbound. Yet, past midnight's veil, by the hearth's gentle fire, her father, John, sat, stoking flames ever higher. A father's plight for his daughter's happiness made building a colony seem trite.

In the glow's tender flicker, he studied the lore, His eyes on the pages learning about America more- it's secrets he'd explore. With a father's devotion, he watched her at rest, A guardian, a sentry, by love's gentle bequest. He was forever chained in love to this life so innocent and pure. He also needed to build a place for her to grow with pleasantries and fur.

His vigil was steadfast, his thoughts ever near, As the night whispered secrets only hearts could hear. His body was there to protect and guide, and outside the door it seemed only demons could hide. His loving gaze cast more than just a net of safety, it drew in a world full of color and wealth in droves that were hefty.

In the cabin's warm haven, by the hearth's steady grace, Silvia's dreams danced, a delicate embrace. With love as their lantern, in the night's gentle flow, Silvia and her father, a bond that would ever grow. Her dreams created energy and magnetism that beckoned in all that surrounded, and turned even the mundane into dancers of light unbounded.

This. This was the American dream, John reflected. If every man, woman, and child could experience what he was experiencing and act in accordance with God's will- this was how men could live in peaceful harmony.

One night, the men of the Mayflower sat down and signed the Mayflower Compact. It was a formal decree stating that the men would submit to God, they would help their neighbor, and they would rule with a democracy.

They held themselves accountable and became a self-governing body in regards to their community. These ideals set the stage for good behavior, no crime, and compassion for each other. It was simple, but the founders believed it was the right thing to do. This decree set the stage for modern American democracy.

In no time in modern history had any group of people gone to such extremes to practice living their faith and freedom. All of these beautiful moments and cherished memories stemmed only from these ideas. After the men reached an understanding, they then began building the community. This took a lot of faith and trust, and they were rewarded handsomely as the future would soon prove. The Pilgrim's named their new colony Plymouth, after the port city they departed from. They wanted to pay homage to their roots so they would have a firm foundation moving forward.

Chapter Three- Rustic Baking

IN PLYMOUTH, THE CHILL of Winter had reigned for many months, its icy grasp keeping the land shrouded in a frosty embrace. The settlers had endured the harshness of the season, their perseverance unwavering as they faced the trials of the New World. The Smith's had caught a huge buck, and the surviving Pilgrim families split it. It was just enough meat to be shredded into their stews for the Winter. Nothing more. Now, as the days grew longer and the sun climbed higher in the sky, a subtle transformation began to stir in the landscape. Animals began to come alive, already looking for the season's first berries. They had weaned themselves off of Mother Earth's bounty before the first snow hit. The time was ripe for filling their empty bodies.

As the snows began to recede, revealing patches of earth beneath, the promise of Spring sprang through the woods. The once-frozen streams trickled with the thaw's reserves, and the air carried the scent of awakening soil and the subtle fragrance of budding life. It was a time of rebirth, of nature rekindling the flame of vitality. It could not be postponed or halted- life was venturing forth with an unwavering hand.

The colonists watched as the trees, which had stood barren for so long, began to unfurl their delicate green leaves, like emerald jewels decorating the woodlands. The meadows transformed, carpeted in wildflowers of luscious colors, a vow of resilience and life would remain everlasting and pure- providing the very cornerstone of hope to the frozen terrain.

Birdsongs, absent in the depths of Winter, returned with a symphony of melodies that filled the air. New songs had been practiced whilst the birds lay dreaming, and finally it was time to sign! The wildlife stirred from their Winter slumber, foraging for the tender shoots that pushed their way through the rich and dense black earth. Nature itself seemed to resonate with the settlers' own sense of renewal.

The people of Plymouth felt the change in their spirits. With the arrival of Spring, their thoughts turned to planting the seeds they had brought with them, sowing the promise of harvest for the future. It was a time of cooperation and shared toil, as the community came together to prepare the land for the bountiful harvests they hoped to reap. The families did not have oxen or cattle at the moment, so they had to settle for hand plowing small plots of land for now. The colony was expecting a small harvest for their first Autumn. Mothers and daughters stayed mainly indoors tending to the babies, the homes, and the meals. They darned the clothes and hung clean laundry out to dry. They happily watched their spouses tend the fields. An onlooker may find them queer to be so glad and jolly. The families could barely hoe a row, and yet they acted like Kings and Queens.

As the world transformed from a monochromatic Winter landscape to a canvas painted with the vibrant hues of Spring, the Pilgrim's found solace in the turning of the seasons. It was a reminder that even in the face of adversity, life would persist, and hope would bloom like the wildflowers in their fields, bringing the promise of a better tomorrow. In the idyllic days of Spring, when the earth was dressed in the green finery of renewal, John and Silvia found respite from their daily toil in the fields of Plymouth. With the seeds planted and their home in the care of the season's warmth, they embarked on a journey of exploration, venturing into the lush meadows and woods that bordered their settlement.

Hand in hand, they strolled through the fields, where wildflowers swayed in the gentle breeze, their colorful petals reaching for the caressing sun. The meadows were a sounding board, alive with the hum of bees and the songs of birds, a chorus of life serenading the world's awakening. Each step they took brought them closer to the chorus. Knowing each other, they felt compelled to beat each other to the position of maestro. Each wanting the honored position of director. They laughed knowing it was never really theirs, and the idea kept their thoughts occupied as they strolled.

Their footsteps, softened by the new grass, took them to the edge of the forest. Beneath the verdant canopy, dappled sunlight played upon the forest floor. Silvia's eyes sparkled with curiosity, and John's steady presence encouraged her to explore the mysteries that lay hidden among the trees. Silvia and John stayed under the protection of Mother Nature's gaze in the wood for hours. Finally, they headed back home.

Under the watchful gaze of the moon, John found solace in the gentle creak of his rocking chair as he settled on the porch of his cabin. It was in the stillness of the night that he allowed himself to confront the complex emotions that had shaped his life in this new land. In the solitude of the wilderness, he could ponder his feelings towards the distant motherland, a place he had left behind in search of freedom and a better life. He knew he was on the right path when he reaffirmed his hunch that Silvia was thriving. When he saw her in the woods, he realized that she was born for adventure. She was sweet and small, but tough and headstrong.

The memories of the Old World, with its challenges and limitations, were never far from his thoughts. He wrestled with the bitterness that sometimes threatened to overtake him, the anger towards a system that had compelled him to leave everything behind. The system that took his beloved spouse. John felt gratitude for being able to even have these thoughts. He realized that Silvia would have suffered the same melancholy- and possibly even the same fate- as her mother had they stayed.

As a single father, he had navigated the turbulent waters of parenthood, and his heart swelled with love and pride for the young girl who was his anchor in this unfamiliar land. It was hard for him to watch his brethren repopulate their colony while he was destined to wander about as the widower that he was. He felt a sting of anger towards God, and he knew he had to repent from the thought immediately or suffer mental anguish. He began rocking in his chair.

The night air seemed to bear witness to his inner struggles, absorbing his thoughts and intentions like a confidant. He thought of his newfound community, the friends he had made, and the bonds that had formed among them. It was in these connections that he discovered a sense of belonging that helped him heal the wounds of the past. He knew he was needed not only for his hard work, his role as a father, but for the neighbor that he was. He helped each one of the family's build their homestead. He helped water their dogs, and take care of minor cuts and bruises. He buried the dead. John needed these reminders of good deeds to build his self-confidence.

With each rocking motion, the rhythm of his contemplation brought a measure of peace. The night's breeze was where he cast his emotions, allowing the darkness to absorb the weight of his sorrows and the warmth of his gratitude and carry it away.

As the hours passed, John found the strength to reconcile with his past and accept the present. And so, under the moon's gentle light, John faced his inner demons, emerging with a heart that was lighter and more resolute, ready to embrace the new dawn of each day in this land that he now called home. He found the place in his body, mind, and soul that needed healing and he focused his energy on these areas. When he finally got up, he was at peace and ready for bed.

As the first rays of daylight pierced through the cabin's wooden shutters, John's eyes fluttered open. His immediate instinct was to check on Silvia, as fathers do when their children are the center of their world. But to his surprise, he found her empty cot, neatly made with care. She silently stayed up last night and watched him rock in his chair. She felt content knowing that he was going to be alright and instantly fell asleep. At dawn's first light, she was so motivated to learn about the land she was occupying, that she practically jumped out of bed.

Alarmed, John leaped to his feet, his concern giving wings to his actions. He hurriedly pulled on his boots and stepped outside. The morning air was crisp and filled with the songs of birds, a stark contrast to the unease that gnawed at his heart. He was not used to the sights and sounds just yet, and it left him a bit off-balance.

It didn't take long for John to spot her. In the distance, he saw Silvia, a tiny figure amidst the lush landscape, moving with a sense of purpose. Her steps were measured, each one bringing her closer to the wild blooms that adorned the meadow. Worry coursed through him, but he knew his daughter's spirit, her boundless curiosity. She was, after all, a reflection of the untamed world they now called home. He only hoped he would take with her the good manners he had instilled in her, so that she could survive any encounters she may stumble upon. Silvia was turning 16 soon, and she was still stuck between a clumsy teenager and a young woman.

Silvia carried in her hand a small notebook, a gift from Matt Brewster, a member of their community known for his knowledge of herbs and healing. It was a simple tool, yet it held the potential to unlock the mysteries of the wilderness. Silvia was on a mission to forage for medicinal herbs and flowers, her quest guided by the wisdom of those who had come before.

John watched her from a distance, torn between the impulse to rush to her side and the realization that she was taking the first steps towards independence. Her earnest demeanor, the way her fingers gently brushed the petals of wildflowers, spoke of an inquisitive spirit.

With every discovery, every entry in her notebook, Silvia was forging a connection to the land and its secrets. The wilderness, with its bountiful offerings and hidden treasures, was her teacher, and the notebook was her scientific journal, upon which she wrote the wisdom of the New World.

As the morning wore on, John's initial anxiety transformed into a quiet pride. Silvia's courage and resourcefulness were a gift to their community, a reflection of the strength that had brought them to this new land.

With a deep breath, John leaned against a tree, his eyes never leaving Silvia's figure in the meadow. In this moment, he found solace in the knowledge that the New World held not only challenges but also opportunities for growth, learning, and the forging of a bond that transcended generations. He let out a tranquil sigh, and prayed that God would keep them this way forever.

Beneath the forest's lush and leafy dome, Silvia ventured, a wanderer far from home. In her hands, a woven basket, empty no more, Filled with herbs and flowers, nature's ancient lore.

Emerging from the canopy's gentle shroud, she danced like a spirit, a presence in the wood, with her heart so light, and her laughter so free, A wildflower nymph, a joyful sight to see. In merriment, she skipped with grace, as sunlight kissed her upturned face. Her eyes aglow with nature's prize, In every herb, in every bloom, life's sweet surprise.

Her father, John, observed her with a loving heart, as Silvia's treasures became a work of art. In her embrace, the forest's gifts took hold, a story of nature's wisdom, beautifully told. With admiration in his steady gaze, he praised her for the knowledge she displayed. In the gentle exchange, a bond did bloom, a shared connection with the earth's perfume.

Through fields and woods, they journeyed on, in the wild heart of their land, where they both belonged. In nature's realm, they walked with grace, Two souls, hand in hand, in an eternal embrace. Father and daughter, in the forest's delight, A love that would endure, through day and night.

One day, as Silvia ventured near the stream's gentle flow, with her blonde hair and petticoats, she moved with a graceful glow, Muddied boots and a spirit so free, nature her closest friend. As she foraged for herbs by the water's serene gleam, a rustling in the brush disrupted her ongoing dream. In the midst of her search, her heart skipped a beat, as she stumbled upon Tautog, a man so strong and neat.

Tautog, fished with skill, where the clear waters gently flowed. Silent and wise, his presence a force of nature's grace, in the tranquil stream, a figure of the wild's dream.

Their paths converged by the stream's serene domain. A moment frozen in time, where worlds did entertain. Silvia, in her petticoats, with innocence so sweet, and Tautog, the fisherman, where nature and hearts would meet. As she stood muddied and curious, her eyes met his gaze. In that silent encounter, a connection did ablaze. Two souls, from different worlds, intertwined by fate, by the stream's flowing rhythm, their destiny would wait.

The Harvest Talisman, warm against Tautog's chest, a sensation profound, like a sacred quest. As he gazed upon Silvia, wonderment in his eyes, he felt the legend's pull, where destiny came alive. In the midst of nature's dance, by the stream they stood, He saw her beauty, like a vision that could capture his heart. An enchanting sight, her doe eyes spoke of wisdom, gentle and bright. Her presence, well-bred and gracefully mild, spoke of an education, nature's favored child. Tautog felt the ancient legend take its course, in her, he saw the future, a mystical force.

As the Harvest Talisman pulsed, the connection grew, their destinies entwined, the legend's promise true, By the stream's timeless flow, in Silvia and Tautog, two hearts, two worlds, became one.

The late morning sun cast long shadows over the rugged, untouched landscape that Tautog called home. He trudged along the rocky shoreline, his fit body absorbing the brunt of the uneven terrain as he made his way back to his wetu. Tautog was a man of few words and even fewer smiles. He had the gruff exterior of someone who had spent his life at the mercy of the sea, but it was his determination and resilience that spoke volumes.

No one on Earth could understand his pain. He was Philip after all, a prince among men. His life was easy and laid back. He had been in the New World for three years now, and nature was wearing him down. He continued walking toward her, making certain to control his movements into an unassuming posture.

Silvia, a newcomer to the land, watched Tautog's approach with wide-eyed wonder. She had arrived from England not too long ago, seeking refuge in this magnificent place. She had never seen a man quite like Tautog before, his rugged features and calloused hands testaments to a life of hard work and unforgiving conditions. She had heard stories of the Native people and their mysterious ways, and now, she found herself face to face with one of them.

As Tautog approached, Silvia shifted her gaze from the fish to his face, her curiosity piqued. She did not know if he would be a violent and angry man or if he would be a gentleman. No matter, she was not expecting him to be a very bright man. His deep-set eyes, like two pieces of obsidian, bore into her with a mixture of scrutiny and guarded interest. Tautog wasn't known for his warm and welcoming demeanor, but Silvia sensed there was more to him than met the eye.

Tautog broke the silence that hung heavy between them, his voice gruff and raspy from years of salt air and sea spray. "What brings you here by the stream, stranger?" he asked, his tone brusque but not unkind. He wanted to know everything about her. He was glad he was able to at least get that question out.

Silvia gathered her thoughts and replied, "I've just moved here from England, and I'm searching for medicinal herbs. The land here is so different from what I'm used to, and I'm still learning its secrets."

Tautog nodded, a faint hint of understanding in his eyes. He had seen many newcomers over the years, each with their own reasons for coming to this rugged land. For most, the challenges were insurmountable, but Silvia's determination intrigued him. He was silently praying she would never leave. These unbearable life circumstances would be manageable if he could just look into her beautiful face and be reminded of his youth with her girlish gait.

"You have a keen eye for plants," he grunted, his rough hand gesturing toward a patch of wildflowers by the stream. He felt as silly as he sounded. "There are medicinal herbs here, but they hide among the others. I can show you what you seek." He was glad he could help navigate her to the information she was searching for. He was thanking his lucky stars his mother had put him in wilderness survival school as a child.

Silvia's eyes lit up with gratitude, and she followed Tautog as he led her deeper into the wilderness. As they walked, he shared his knowledge of the land, its hidden treasures, and the ways of his people. He was trying to cover a lot of ground to get to a certain level of respect for his new companion. Silvia listened with rapt attention, realizing that beneath Tautog's gruff exterior lay a wealth of wisdom and a genuine willingness to help. She desperately wanted to remember everything he said and she was kicking herself for not writing any of it down. Her only hope was that he would repeat himself at another point in time. She smiled happily at him as she followed him down the stream.

As Tautog and Silvia continued their walk through the dense woods, his long strides and purposeful positioning made it evident that he was a man who knew these paths well. The rugged terrain posed little challenge for him, and his boots navigated the uneven ground with ease. Silvia, on the other hand, found herself having to jog occasionally to keep up with his self-inflicted pace. Her youthful energy, in stark contrast to Tautog's seasoned endurance, was evident in the way she bounced along, trying to match his steps.

Silvia couldn't help but admire the maturity and wisdom that radiated from Tautog. His years of living off the land and facing the untamed wilderness had bore lines of experience onto his face. His broad shoulders, scarred by the struggles of his people, bore the weight of his responsibilities with unwavering strength. He had more healed wounds than he knew what to do with, given all of the manual labor he had subjected himself to during his stay with the Herring Pond tribe.

With every step, Silvia stole glances at Tautog. She marveled at the knowledge he possessed, not just of the land but of the world beyond it. As a newcomer from England, she was constantly learning, adapting, and seeking guidance from those who had lived in this harsh environment for generations. Tautog, in his gruff yet reliable manner, was a man she looked up to. Her mind simply could not wrap around everything he was telling her, and her impatience with herself to truly understand all that he was saying gnawed at her like a giant werewolf from her childhood stories. She reminded herself to stay calm and persevere.

"I have to get back to the tribe, now." Tautog told her. He went to move a branch out of her path, and she ran squarely into his hard and muscular body. She looked down embarrassed. Instinctively, he bent down and cradled her face in his hands. They shared a moment of togetherness and comfort in each other's care. Startled by their ease around each other, they looked away and began walking again.

"I come to this stream often to fish. My tribe knows quite a bit about herbs, would you like to come and talk about it another time?" Tautog inquired. Silvia was still reeling from being touched in such an intimate way. She was also impressed by his ability to speak English, however accented it may be.

"Y...yes. I would love that." She replied.

"Great, meet me here tomorrow at dawn." He walked on, giving her a warm smile over his shoulder as he strutted away. Tautog had become Silvia's first friend.

Tautog picked up a bundle of freshly caught fish in one arm and a net slung over his shoulder, secured by a rough-hewn strap made of braided vines. The fish were a welcome sight, and he could feel the eyes of his fellow tribespeople watching as he approached. The tribe had been sparse in recent years, and every catch was a precious bounty that would help sustain them through the harsh New England seasons.

In the coming weeks, Silvia and Tautog forged an unexpected friendship. She learned the art of foraging for herbs and healing plants, and he, in turn, discovered a kindred spirit in this resilient newcomer from across the ocean. Together, they uncovered the secrets of the land, finding beauty and solace in its untamed wilderness, and slowly but surely, Tautog's gruff exterior began to soften in the presence of Silvia's unwavering curiosity and gratitude. He could hardly believe he found love. He knew she was young and he promised himself he would wait for her for however long he needed to.

Silvia kept her blossoming friendship with Tautog a well-guarded secret from her father. The routines of her new life in the colony were defined by her father's expectations. On weekdays, she was required to attend school in a one-room schoolhouse, where she diligently studied, learned the ways of the land, and fostered friendships with the other children. Sundays were dedicated to church services, which were held in a makeshift church, and Silvia participated in the religious activities with devotion.

While Silvia embraced the structure and sense of community that her father had introduced into her life, she continued to hold onto her morning meetings with Tautog. These early meetings by the stream became her own personal sanctuary, a brief escape from the structured world of her father's making. Silvia had developed a deep passion for the herbs and medicinal plants that the New England wilderness had to offer, and Tautog was her most valued mentor in this regard.

In the quiet moments shared by the stream, Tautog passed down his knowledge of the land to Silvia. He taught her the names, properties, and uses of various herbs and plants, drawing on centuries of wisdom passed down through generations. As they examined leaves, stems, and roots, their friendship deepened, and Silvia felt like she was becoming a part of his very personality. He was never out of surprises for her. Some days it was a special root, a flower, or a trinket made by members of his tribe. He never got tired of watching her light up with delight.

Despite the secrecy surrounding their relationship, Silvia treasured her time with Tautog. The practical lessons she received from the ladies in the colony about becoming a woman were complemented by the knowledge she gained from Tautog about the land and its bounty. It was as if she was learning to become a woman in two distinct worlds: one defined by the structured society her father sought to establish, and the other, a more ancient and natural world guided by the wisdom of her Native friend.

As time passed, Silvia's life in the colony continued to evolve, but her meetings with Tautog remained a constant, hidden thread connecting her to a deeper, more primal understanding of the land and the people who had lived on it for generations.

Silvia's desire to introduce her father, John, to Tautog had been growing stronger with each passing day. She believed that bringing these two important figures in her life together could bridge the gap between her old world and the new one she had come to embrace. Tautog, too, felt a similar yearning. He wanted to share the young Englishwoman who had become a dear friend with the women of his tribe, to show them the beauty of her spirit and her deep reverence for the land.

One clear, brisk morning, Silvia approached her father with her proposal, her heart pounding with anticipation. "Father, I would like you to meet Tautog," she said with a mixture of excitement and trepidation. "He is a friend of mine and a wise man of the tribe. I believe you would learn much from him, just as I have."

John looked at his daughter with a curious expression, her request giving him pause. He had built a new life for them in this colony, a life he had envisioned with certain values and principles. The idea of opening up their world to someone so different from what he had known made him uneasy. It also riled him up that a grown man would feel comfortable spending time with a young girl alone. He tried not to let his disdain for this stranger to show.

Silvia could see the hesitation in her father's eyes and decided to elaborate, attempting to bridge the gap between their two worlds. "Father, Tautog is a man of great wisdom and experience," she continued. "He has taught me about the land and its medicinal herbs, and I've learned so much from him. He said I made him realize he has put up walls. He said I strip them down like varnish from a hull. He said I put the electricity in his motor most days." She looked at her father with questioning eyes. She had no idea what electricity was, let alone a motor.

John raised an eyebrow, recognizing the distinct reference from his daughter's words. It was a stark contrast to the language he was accustomed to hearing. The mention of electricity in a motor struck a cord with him. These inventions were being thought of, but had not come to fruition. John knew he needed to meet Tautog. He let his negative feelings go and began to focus on just who this Tautog was.

"Silvia, you have a way of seeing the world that's beyond my understanding," John admitted with a mixture of admiration and concern. "But I trust your judgment, and if this Tautog is as wise as you say, then I am willing to meet him."

Silvia's eyes lit up with joy at her father's agreement. She knew this was a significant step toward merging their two worlds, and it was a testament to John's love for her. She made the arrangements for Tautog to meet her father, and in a few days, they gathered at a designated spot near the stream.

When Tautog and John came face to face, there was an unspoken tension between them. John's presence and the world he represented were unfamiliar to Tautog, and likewise, John couldn't help but wonder about the mysterious man who had captured his daughter's heart. The meeting was a collision of two worlds. Tautog remained unflustered, an air of superiority about him. John humbled himself to this gentle Native man.

As they exchanged greetings, the conversation remained polite, but the undercurrent of curiosity and uncertainty was palpable. Tautog and John were about to embark on a journey that would challenge their preconceived notions and open their eyes to the complexities of the world and the people in it. John noted that Tautog spoke excellent English, sometimes using words and phrases that were even more complex than John's typical vocabulary. He had to fight of feelings of intimidation so he could truly learn from this majestic man.

As Tautog guided John and Silvia back to his camp, they followed a winding path through the dense forest, the air filled with the earthy scent of pine and the soft rustling of leaves. The camp, nestled near the waterfront, came into view, a collection of modest wigwams and a central fire pit, where a fire burned steadily. The tribe's Chief, a dignified figure with weathered features and adorned in traditional garments, sat by the fire with Squanto, a native who had learned to speak a different dialect of English through his interactions with European settlers.

Tautog and Squanto exchanged greetings in their shared language, a testament to their adaptability and their understanding of the need to bridge cultural gaps. For John, this was a profound moment of gratitude, as it meant he could communicate and understand the people of this land more easily. He had been apprehensive about this visit, but now he felt a sense of camaraderie. He was in no way physically fit enough to fight anyone off, and now he was certain he was not smarter than these men. His faith, however, shown forth like a beam of energy that all could appreciate.

After the initial greetings, Silvia was guided to the kitchen area where the women of the tribe had gathered to prepare food. Silvia's eyes sparkled with curiosity as she explored the cooking methods, ingredients, and culinary traditions that were so different from what she knew back in England. She quickly made herself useful, assisting the women in their tasks and, in turn, learning from their expertise. The women were caught off guard by her eagerness to learn. They joyfully held her back from their creations, and walked her slowly into their culinary dance.

Meanwhile, the men sat around the fire, the flames casted dancing shadows on their faces. Tautog and John, despite their different backgrounds and worlds, found themselves engaged in a conversation that transcended language and culture. They shared stories of their experiences, their struggles, and their visions for the future of this land.

Tautog spoke of the sea, the bountiful catch of fish, and the challenges his people faced. He shared tales of survival, the wisdom passed down from their ancestors, and the bond his tribe had with the land and its resources. John, in turn, spoke of his dreams for the colony, his hope for cooperation with the native people, and his desire to build a prosperous and peaceful community.

Around the fire, the two men found common ground in their shared desire for a better future. It was a simple yet powerful connection, rooted in the recognition that, despite their differences, they were all part of this untamed land. They had so much to teach each other, and both were excited to learn as much as possible for their own survival, as well as for their people. The fire's warmth and the camaraderie that developed between Tautog and John served as a symbol of the potential for unity and cooperation in the face of the unknown challenges that lay ahead.

Over the passing of seasons, like the pages of a richly woven tapestry, Silvia's visits to Tautog's camp became a cherished ritual. In the heart of the wilderness, amid the embrace of nature's beauty, she discovered a hidden passion, a symphony of flavors waiting to be composed in the rustic kitchen of the tribe. She noticed that the crops her family planted in the Spring never grew. The seeds they had brought with them on the Mayflower were not fertile and did not produce a crop. She was thankful for the ability to cook and learn with the food the tribe had provided.

Her eager spirit, undaunted by the unfamiliar ingredients and techniques, took on a new purpose. It was through the humble pumpkin that she began her culinary journey. Silvia learned to peel away the tough exterior, revealing the vibrant orange flesh within. With deft hands, she sliced and diced, transforming the vegetable into fragrant chunks that promised warmth and comfort.

The spices, a medley of aromas and colors, held the secret to flavor. Cinnamon, nutmeg, and cloves whispered tales of far-off lands, while ginger and allspice added their exotic notes to the pot. Silvia's delicate touch measured these aromatic treasures, creating an enchanting blend that would infuse her dishes with character and depth.

The fire crackled, its dancing flames casting flickering shadows on the kitchen walls. Silvia stirred the bubbling pot with a wooden spoon, the steam carrying the tantalizing promise of what was to come. With each passing day, her confidence grew, and she learned to balance the flavors, to know when to add more warmth or sweetness, creating culinary masterpieces that transcended cultural boundaries.

Her palate, once attuned to the restrained and formal tastes of her homeland, expanded. She marveled at the fusion of the old world and the new, where English sensibilities mingled with the wild and untamed flavors of the New England wilderness. Silvia's culinary creations were a testament to her adaptability, her open-hearted exploration of a foreign culture, and her growing expertise as a cook.

Season after season, her passion blossomed, and Silvia became renowned among the tribe for her exceptional skills. She embraced the role of a bridge between her world and theirs, a culinary ambassador who brought warmth and flavor to the table, forging connections that transcended language and culture.

Tautog's role as Silvia's protector and mentor became a fundamental part of their unique relationship. As the seasons passed and Silvia continued her visits to Tautog's camp, he watched over her with a sense of guardianship that transcended words. It was as though he had taken on the role of a silent sentinel, ensuring that Silvia felt safe and supported in this new and untamed world.

Whenever Silvia had questions about the land, its flora and fauna, or the customs of Tautog's people, he was there, ready to share his wisdom. He answered her inquiries patiently, explaining the nuances of the wilderness and the ancestral knowledge that had sustained his tribe for generations. His deep connection to the land and its history provided Silvia with a wellspring of understanding.

Tautog's protective instincts extended beyond answering questions. He was quick to intervene and mediate any misunderstandings that arose between Silvia and the members of his tribe. His presence served as a bridge between her world and theirs, a reassuring presence that smoothed the path of cultural exchange and mutual respect.

John, Silvia's father, often observed Tautog and Silvia's connection with a sense of wonder and curiosity. He had initially been wary of this mysterious Native man who had entered their lives. As he witnessed the bond between Tautog and his daughter grow, he couldn't help but feel a growing appreciation for the depth of their friendship.

John was moved by the way Tautog looked after Silvia, offering her guidance and protection. He saw their connection as a testament to the potential for unity and cooperation between their two worlds, and it challenged his preconceived notions. As he looked over Tautog's shoulder, he saw a friendship that transcended language and culture, and it filled him with a newfound sense of hope and understanding. It was a platonic and helpful relationship, and John was proud that Silvia had the nerve to befriend this man in the first place.

Silvia's culinary prowess, nurtured and refined through her visits to Tautog's camp, became a source of wonder and admiration among the Native women. Her ability to transform humble ingredients into delectable dishes was nothing short of enchanting, and her influence was impossible to ignore. As word spread of her culinary talents, the Native women couldn't help but feel a pang of jealousy.

In their eyes, Silvia had become an intriguing figure, the outsider who had seamlessly embraced their traditions and elevated them to new heights. They watched her work with spices, herbs, and locally-sourced ingredients, weaving a tapestry of flavors that not only delighted the palate but also hinted at the promise of cultural fusion. Her skills seemed to transcend the boundaries of their Native cuisine, and the women couldn't help but be entranced by the culinary magic she conjured.

The green-eyed embers of jealousy smoldered as the women observed how the men in the tribe, particularly Tautog, were drawn to Silvia's cooking like moths to a flame. Her meals became a magnet that drew people to her, and the communal aspect of sharing a meal with Silvia was a powerful force that couldn't be denied. The Native women began to feel a sense of displacement, their traditional roles overshadowed by the presence of this skilled and charismatic newcomer.

One evening, as the sun set over the camp, John and Silvia had a candid conversation about the growing tension. It was evident that Silvia's culinary skills were causing unrest among the women, and John didn't want to further strain their already delicate relationship with the tribe. They decided on a compromise: Silvia would stay home, and the Native Americans would be invited to her to taste her cooking from then on.

This decision was met with mixed emotions. The Native women, on one hand, felt a sense of relief as the source of their unease was removed. On the other hand, they couldn't help but wonder if Silvia's culinary creations would continue to captivate and influence their tribe, even from a distance.

Silvia's kitchen, now transformed into a hub of cross-cultural exchange, remained a place of connection and understanding. While the Native women may have felt a tinge of jealousy, Silvia's love for the land and her respect for their traditions allowed her to share her culinary passion and bring people together in a spirit of unity. The path to acceptance and cooperation was fraught with challenges, but they were challenges worth overcoming for the sake of building a harmonious community in this new society.

In the dappled light of the early evening, Tautog's visits to Silvia's cabin were a quiet, harmonious symphony of nature and friendship. With every step he took through the lush forest, he carried with him a bouquet of medicinal flowers, a gesture that bridged the gap between their worlds, a silent testament to their deep bond.

As he approached the cabin, the scent of the forest clung to him, an earthy perfume that spoke of the untamed land he called home.

The wooden door, well-worn and welcoming, swung open to reveal the cozy warmth of Silvia's cabin. The air inside was filled with the aroma of simmering herbs and spices, a promise of a meal that would soon be shared.

Silvia, with her eyes bright and a smile gracing her lips, welcomed Tautog into her home. The medicinal flowers he brought were not just symbols of healing; they were tokens of their enduring friendship, a reminder of the lessons learned and the stories shared in the heart of the wilderness.

They settled in the living room, a space where cultures intertwined. The flickering flames of the hearth cast dancing shadows on the wooden walls, and the comfortable chairs, adorned with handwoven textiles, cradled their bodies like ancient storytellers.

Silvia, with her culinary artistry and a deep respect for the land, created a shared feast that transcended boundaries. A harmonious fusion of ingredients from her homeland and the Native flavors she had embraced, the meal was a testament to the potential for unity and understanding.

The conversation flowed like a gentle stream, weaving between the past and the present. They spoke not only of the land, but also of the intricate workings of the human mind, of the advances in modern psychology. Tautog's wisdom and insight were like treasures unearthed from the depths of experience, each word a pearl of profound knowledge that illuminated the room.

John, the father who had once been wary of Tautog's presence, found himself drawn into the conversation, his skepticism replaced by a deep respect for the Native man's wisdom. Tautog's words, filled with the wisdom of the land and the wisdom of the human spirit, held a magnetic power that captivated all who listened. It was as though the walls of the cabin disappeared, and they sat as a family, a united front, bound by the common pursuit of understanding and cooperation.

When it was time to sit down and enjoy Silvia's food, Tautog teased John about his small harvest. John understood that Toutog was just poking a bit of fun, and John slowly at until his belly was full. He appreciated these young kids looking out for him, including him, and feeding him. While Tautog and Silvia had been busy at the tribe's camp, John was busy making contracts in Jamestown for fencing, livestock, and tools.

It was in these moments of shared knowledge and direction, that John and Tautog worked out an agreement between the colony and the tribe. They formed an alliance and made a treaty, the Treaty of Tordesillas, which Tautog took back to Chief Massasoit and Squanto. The tribal leaders agreed to the treaty as did the colony founders. The treaty stated that there would be no weapons at their meetings, no one would steal from another without being punished, and finally, that they would not harm each other.

The Native people had been through a lot in the past three years, and they could really use a morally-sound family to stabilize and strengthen them. They had no idea what most of the White men were talking about, and Tautog and Squanto spent the majority of their time explaining European behaviors and attitudes.

The Pilgrims were also a bit fearful of the men that lived on the land. The Natives seemed welcoming and inviting enough. The Pilgrim's decided to live in harmony with them, even though they did not share the same culture or belief system. They believed that in time, all would reach an equilibrium and that peace would win over any disagreement or argument. After this new treaty was formed, the two cultures were ready to learn from each other.

In a distant land across the sea, Squanto's story began, A Native of the Patuxet tribe, with a tale marred by sins. Kidnapped by Englishmen, in a land far from his own, taken to London's bustling streets, a place he hadn't known. In the heart of England's city, far from Native soil, Squanto learned a foreign tongue, a life of ceaseless toil. He served his captors and absorbed their ways, but memories of his homeland, in his heart, persuaded.

Years passed, and Squanto yearned for home, the land of heart's desire, He longed for Plymouth's rocky shore, a place to reacquire. Yet when he returned to native shores, the world had changed so much, Disease and conflict had taken toll, leaving little left to touch. Squanto, wise and resilient, held on to what he knew, He taught the Pilgrims how to plant corn, in the hopes that they'd construe, the land belonged to no one, it was a gift for all to share, a lesson rooted deep within him, a wisdom strong and rare.

With a stick and a fish, he showed the way to till, He taught them of the Three Sisters, a harmonious skill. Corn, beans, and squash, their roots deep in the earth, In this lesson of the land, Squanto's true worth. The Pilgrims watched in wonder as he demonstrated the lore, He explained that all could prosper, that there was room for more. The land, he said, belongs to none, but to all who till its soil, a shared gift from the earth, a truth to mend and toil.

Squanto's teachings sparked a unity, a bond in Plymouth's clay, As the Pilgrims and the Natives, side by side, toiled away. The land belonged to no one, a lesson strong and true, A shared vision of the future, as the harvest season grew. Squanto, a Native son, with wisdom in his hand, Taught the Pilgrims how to farm, to till the Native land. His methods were a revelation, their old ways could not suffice, He showed them secrets of the earth, how to grow and reap their rice.

For Tautog, with his skillful hands, also shared what he had seen. He taught the Pilgrims how to fish, using methods born of here, In the New World's vast bounty, they'd find a way to persevere. The Pilgrims, once beholden to their old world's ways, now embraced the teachings of their friends in these new days. For in the fusion of their knowledge, a brighter path did gleam, a testament to unity, a dream of the American dream.

In Squanto's teachings and Tautog's craft, they found the way ahead, Farming and fishing, side by side, their new lives to be led. The land, once shrouded in mystery, had secrets to unroll, In the wisdom of these new friends, they found a common goal. The Pilgrims and their Native guides, together hand in hand, learned to navigate the challenges of the land.

The Pilgrim's exchanged wisdom with the Native Americans. They taught the tribe about plowing and introduced them to grain, wheat, cattle, pigs, and poultry. The Pilgrim's loved discussing animal husbandry to their new family. They also brought along metal tools, trade goods, and fortified housing. They spoke of Christianity, and brought it to many tribes.

As the seasons unfolded in the New World, Silvia and Tautog's friendship continued to flourish. The bond they shared grew stronger with each passing day, and it was marked by a spirit of mutual learning and cultural exchange. Silvia, who had been introduced to new skills and techniques by the Pilgrims, now found herself in a role of teaching and sharing her knowledge with Tautog.

One crisp morning, as the sun cast its golden glow over the land, Silvia decided it was time to show Tautog the wonders of metal tools. She had observed the Native man using his expertly crafted stone and wooden implements for various tasks, but she believed that the introduction of metal tools could make many of his daily tasks easier.

Tautog had always been a keen observer, plus he was from the future where his favorite metal tool was the fork. He welcomed Silvia's initiative with curiosity and an open heart. She led him to the small workshop in her cabin where a modest collection of metal tools lay, each one gleaming in the morning light. The room was adorned with the warmth of wood and the scent of freshly worked metal.

Silvia picked up a simple iron knife and showed Tautog how it could cut through vegetables with ease, its sharp edge a stark contrast to the stone blades he was accustomed to. She then demonstrated the use of a metal spade, how it could dig deep into the earth, turning the soil for planting with less effort than wooden tools. Tautog watched with fascination. He enjoyed being near her more than the dry and informational demonstrations she led.

The exchange of knowledge between the Pilgrims and Tautog's tribe had opened new horizons for both communities. As the seasons turned, the time came when John, Silvia's father, sought to share one of the essential skills from the Pilgrims' world – animal husbandry.

The Pilgrims had brought livestock with them on the Mayflower, and they recognized that animal husbandry could be a valuable addition to the Native way of life. John approached Tautog's tribe with a proposal to introduce them to the raising of livestock, explaining the benefits of having animals for food, labor, and resources.

Tautog, with his characteristic wisdom and openness, welcomed the idea. He understood that the exchange of knowledge was a two-way street, and just as the Pilgrims had learned from the Natives, the Native people could benefit from the Pilgrims' expertise.

The tribe gathered to hear John's teachings, and together, they embarked on a journey of learning. John explained how to build sturdy structures to house the livestock, demonstrating the construction of wooden stables. The Native people were intrigued by these new methods, so different from their own traditional dwellings. Silvia enjoyed volunteering her time to help her friends thrive. She spent many hours playing with the children and teaching them English as they fed the livestock.

With John's guidance, they set to work building fortified structures, incorporating some elements from the Pilgrims' style of construction. The buildings were designed to protect the animals from the harsh New England weather and potential threats from predators. This construction was a collaborative effort, with the Pilgrims and Native people working side by side to create something new and practical.

Fences were erected to create enclosures for the animals, a concept foreign to the Native tribes. John explained the importance of maintaining these boundaries to ensure the safety and well-being of the livestock. Silvia, who had learned from her father, played an active role in teaching the Native women the proper care and feeding of the animals.

The tribe's transformation was evident in their determination to embrace these new practices. As they continued to work on the buildings and fences, they shared their knowledge of the land, its seasons, and its flora with the Pilgrims. The exchange of wisdom created a sense of unity and mutual respect, and the fortified buildings and animal husbandry practices became a symbol of their shared journey.

While they waited for their crops to grow, the tribe and the Pilgrims found purpose in building a future together, one that harmonized their worlds in new and meaningful ways. The fortified buildings and fences stood as a testament to their evolving culture, a fusion of traditions that demonstrated the potential for unity and cooperation in the heart of the New World.

The bond between Tautog and Silvia continued to deepen, as did their mutual respect for each other's beliefs and traditions. As they sat by the fire on many a quiet evening, their friendship allowed for the exchange of knowledge, stories, and, in Tautog's case, a growing curiosity about Christianity.

Tautog had admired Silvia's discipline and her unwavering commitment to her Christian faith. He was curious about the teachings of Jesus and the stories she shared about the life and message of the Savior. With a heart open to understanding, Tautog found himself drawn to the warmth of the fire and the wisdom of Silvia's words. She lived everyday as if it were her last, and Tautog admired this about her. If he could learn just this teaching from Christianity, then he was converted!

One evening, as the embers crackled and the stars sparkled overhead, Tautog turned to Silvia and asked a question that had been on his mind for some time. "Silvia," he began, his voice filled with genuine curiosity, "can you tell me more about this Jesus you speak of? What were His teachings, and why is He so important to your faith?"

Silvia, who had been patient in sharing her faith, was pleased by Tautog's interest. She smiled and replied, "Of course, Tautog. Jesus is central to Christianity. He taught us to love one another, to be compassionate and kind, and to care for those in need. He performed miracles, such as healing the sick and feeding the hungry. His life and sacrifice are seen as a means of redemption and forgiveness for our sins."

Tautog listened intently, absorbing the teachings and stories with an open heart. He asked more questions, seeking to understand the significance of Jesus in Silvia's faith. "And what about this concept of forgiveness?" he inquired. "How does it work in your faith?"

Silvia nudged him playfully and explained, "Forgiveness is a fundamental principle in Christianity. We believe that through faith in Jesus, our sins can be forgiven, and we can find salvation and eternal life. It means letting go of anger and resentment and seeking reconciliation with others and with God. Jesus taught us to forgive others as we hope to be forgiven ourselves."

Tautog nodded, his eyes reflecting his deep contemplation. The teachings of Jesus were new and intriguing to him, offering a perspective on life and faith that differed from his own Native traditions. Their conversations by the fireside became a journey of spiritual discovery for both of them, as Tautog learned about Christianity. It was Silvia's turn to learn about his Native faith.

He took both of her hands in his. He knew she instinctually understood his beliefs. He wanted to provide comfort to her knowing that most of her family was half a world away. They said a prayer for her mother, and she got up to go home. "Thank you for sharing with me." Tautog called after her. Wiping a tear from her eye, she smiled and headed home.

Through their shared moments of questioning, listening, and learning, their friendship blossomed, and they discovered that understanding and respect could flourish even in the face of cultural and spiritual differences. The firelight that illuminated their conversations represented the warmth of their friendship and the power of shared experiences to bridge the gap between their worlds.

In the heart of a world untamed, they met, Silvia and Tautog, their souls were set. A friendship kindled in the wilderness wild, two worlds intertwined, where dreams beguiled. Tautog, rugged, with eyes like the deep, admired Silvia, her secrets to keep. Unrequited love, a silent ember's glow, a longing heart, yet he chose not to show.

He walked beside her, his heart in disguise, yearning for moments, his love in his eyes. A desire to be close, to hold her near, but the chasm of cultures, a barrier to clear. They laughed by the firelight, shared stories untold, In the night's tender embrace, a connection to hold. Tautog longed for more, for their spirits to meet, but the world and its boundaries kept love's dance fleet.

In the depths of the forest, where whispers of trees, revealed ancient secrets carried on the breeze. Their friendship was sacred, a treasure profound, Silvia and Tautog, on hallowed ground. In the heart of the New World, where cultures did blend, Silvia and Tautog, like kin and like friend. A bond that transcended, their love undefined, in the language of friendship, their hearts intertwined.

In the heart of the wilderness, where knowledge and wisdom intertwined, Silvia and John embarked on a journey to help Tautog find mental clarity and focus. They respected the Native ways; however, they had the suspicion that Tautog was a prophet or time traveler. Their own understanding of herbal remedies led them to craft a special concoction.

They gathered herbs and plants native to the land, each one chosen for its unique properties. The star of their herbal remedy was the vibrant blue cohosh, known for its potential to enhance cognitive function and improve mental clarity. They mixed it with ginseng, renowned for its revitalizing qualities, and yarrow, believed to promote mental acuity.

Silvia and John dried and ground the herbs, then carefully combined them in precise proportions. The result was a fragrant herbal blend, with hints of earthiness and the forest's essence. Tautog was introduced to their remedy, and he approached it with an open heart. Silvia explained the intended benefits, and John described their deep respect for the native traditions, emphasizing that their aim was to share knowledge and help, not to impose their beliefs.

As Tautog embraced this new concoction, the aroma of the forest's gifts filled the air. The blend of herbs was a testament to the bond between cultures, a symbol of unity, and the potential for shared wisdom to bring clarity and understanding.

Over time, Tautog felt the subtle effects of the herbal remedy, as his thoughts became clearer, his focus sharper, and his connection with Silvia and John deepened. It was a blend of knowledge and friendship, a testament to the beauty of different worlds coming together to create something meaningful in the heart of the New World. In time, Tautog would begin to explain as best he could the very physics of time travel.

In the heart of a cabin, by the hearth's warm embrace, Silvia prepared a pumpkin pie, a smile on her face. The aroma of spices filled the air, a sweet delight, as she worked with tender hands, in the soft candlelight. The pumpkin, tender and orange, a gift from the earth, Silvia's culinary artistry, a touch of her worth. With a rolling pin and gentle grace, she shaped the dough, a promise of a delicious treat, a love to bestow.

Tautog watched her skillfully, admiration in his eyes, Silvia's mastery of cooking, a wondrous surprise. The crust, golden and flaky, like the sun's own glow, wrapped around the pumpkin, where the flavors would flow. John, from his rocking chair, observed with delight, His daughter's culinary gift, a beautiful sight. The bonds of love and family, as strong as the oak, in the heart of the cabin, where cherished memories spoke.

As the pie baked to perfection, the sweet scent did rise, Silvia's pumpkin masterpiece, a feast for the skies. In that cozy cabin, by the fire's warm influence, they shared a moment to remember, a family surrendered.

As the moon hung low in the night sky, Tautog began his journey back to his tribe's camp after a pleasant evening spent at John's cabin. The path through the woods was familiar to him, the same path he had tread many times before, and the cool, crisp air was a comforting motivator.

However, as he walked deeper into the forest, he was suddenly accosted by a couple of Pilgrims who had been lurking in the shadows. Their intentions were far from friendly, and they began to taunt and harass him about his relationship with Silvia, fueling their words with misunderstanding and hostility. The night took a sinister turn, as he did not feel the need to defend his relationships to anyone.

The Pilgrims' words stung, but he held his ground, his face marked with determination and a resolute spirit. As the confrontation escalated, Tautog's hand instinctively found a sturdy rock on the forest floor. With a swift and powerful motion, he hurled the rock toward his harassers, landing a powerful blow that startled them into a momentary retreat.

In the moment of chaos and confusion, Tautog seized the opportunity to break free from their grasp. He ran through the darkened woods, his heart pounding and his breath quickened, determined to return to his tribe's camp and put distance between himself and the hostile Pilgrims.

His escape through the dense forest and the memory of that harrowing encounter would serve as a stark reminder of the challenges and misunderstandings that still existed between their two worlds, even as the bonds of friendship and unity continued to grow.

In the solitude of the forest, Tautog found a quiet refuge by the stream, where the glistening waters whispered soothing secrets to his wounded soul. The encounter with the hostile Pilgrims had left him battered and bruised, his spirit aching with the weight of their words.

As he sat by the stream, the gentle murmur of water played a comforting lullaby, and Tautog's thoughts drifted to his family, his mother and father, who were no longer by his side. A wave of longing washed over him, and tears began to flow, mingling with the rivulets of the stream.

In his moment of vulnerability, Tautog felt the weight of isolation, the sense of being adrift in a sea of misunderstanding. He yearned for the warm embrace of his parents, for their wisdom, their help, and the sense of belonging they had always provided.

But then, like a whisper in the breeze, the story of Jesus that Silvia had shared came to him. He remembered the teachings of love, compassion, and forgiveness. He thought of the sacrifices that had been made for the greater good, and the message of healing and redemption.

With newfound strength welling up within him, Tautog realized that forgiveness was the path he needed to tread. He found the courage to release the anger and hurt that had consumed him, to let go of the darkness that the encounter had left behind. In the power of forgiveness, Tautog found his way back home, not just to his tribe's camp but to a place of inner peace.

As he rested among his people, his spirit renewed and his heart lighter, Tautog knew that the encounter with the Pilgrims had been a test of character, a challenge to find the courage to forgive and let go. In that moment, by the stream and under the guidance of a story shared, Tautog discovered the strength to move forward, bridging the gap between two worlds with a heart that bore the weight of understanding and a soul willing to embrace forgiveness.

In the heart of the night, as Tautog lay in his wetu, thoughts of Silvia filled his mind. Her wisdom, her friendship, and her unwavering kindness had been a guiding light in his life, and he realized that his feelings for her ran deeper than he had ever acknowledged. Silvia had shared the teachings of her faith, her stories by the fireside, and her compassion in times of need. Tautog found himself grateful for her presence, for the lessons they had shared, and for the way she had opened his heart to new horizons.

In the stillness of the night, as the moonlight cast a gentle glow, Tautog's talisman, a cherished token of his heritage, began to burn brightly. It felt as though the passion in his heart had ignited a powerful flame within him, and that fire spread through his entire being. He realized that he loved Silvia, a love as profound as the ancient forest and as powerful as the river's flow. The realization was both an awakening and a revelation, a truth that had lain dormant within him for too long.

As the talisman glowed, he understood that, like the talisman, their connection was something sacred and enduring, a force that had the power to bridge the gap between their two cultures. In that moment of realization, Tautog's heart blazed with a fierce and gentle passion, a flame of love that had the potential to illuminate their shared path and define the future of their friendship. Silvia's teachings and their enduring bond had brought him to this profound moment, and he felt both humbled and blessed to carry this newfound love within him.

The following morning, Tautog arose with a sense of stiffness in his limbs and a noticeable bruise on his arm, a poignant reminder to the challenges of the previous day. The physical toll of their daily life as fishermen and the occasional confrontations with Pilgrims had left its mark on him.

Recognizing the need to address his injuries, the women of the tribe came to his aid. With a gentle touch and a wealth of knowledge passed down through generations, they prepared a healing concoction using the yucca plant. Yucca was a versatile plant with natural cleansing properties, making it an ideal choice for disinfecting and soothing wounds.

They ground the yucca roots and leaves, creating a lather that would help cleanse and disinfect Tautog's body. As they applied the lather to his wounds, the cool sensation of the yucca provided relief, and its natural properties helped reduce inflammation and promote healing.

After the initial care, Tautog sought further respite to aid his recovery. He made his way to a nearby hot spring, a natural wonder that held the power to soothe aching muscles and promote healing. The warm, mineral-rich waters enveloped him, easing the tension in his body and allowing him to relax and find solace in the embrace of nature.

Resting in the hot spring, Tautog contemplated the events of the past days. He knew that the path to unity and understanding between his people and the Pilgrims was not without its challenges. The healing rituals, the wisdom of the women, and the serene hot spring were reminders of the importance of caring for oneself and each other in the face of adversity.

Chapter Four- The First Thanksgiving

AS THE SUN PAINTED the sky with hues of dawn, Tautog awoke with the memories of his past Thanksgiving gently woven through his dreams. The recollections of shared laughter, the unity of cultures, and the warmth of his mother filled his heart with a sense of gratitude. These memories were cherished, precious like a gleaming ray of light against a crystal.

He began his day by making his way to the stream, a familiar and sacred place for cleansing and reflection. The rippling waters mirrored the changing seasons, and the morning light danced upon the surface, a reminder of the endless cycle of life. At the stream, other tribal members were already present, going about their morning routines. Tautog greeted them with a nod, and they exchanged thoughts about the warmer weather that was beginning to grace their land. The coming of Spring was a time of promise and renewal, a season that held the potential for new growth, bountiful harvests, and fresh beginnings.

As they washed and gathered water, they pondered what the changing season would bring this year. Would the fields yield a rich harvest? Would the forests offer their treasures, and would the rivers be generous with their bounty? In the heart of the tribe's shared hopes, there was a sense of anticipation and unity, much like the bonds they had formed with the Pilgrims.

Tautog felt the warmth of their community and the presence of his ancestors in the gentle caress of the wind. He let the soap lather and rinse away. The women seemed more interested than he once thought. The memories of Thanksgiving were a reminder that despite the differences and misunderstandings that sometimes arose, there was also a profound sense of togetherness and shared blessings. He felt a bit uneasy as he continued to wash.

As the members of the tribe gathered at the stream, their faces aglow with the promise of a new day, Tautog's mind was brimming with a multitude of ideas, innovations, and dreams. He felt a deep connection to the land, the traditions of his people, and the emerging potential for their tribe's future. With the warm sun on his face and the ripple of the stream's water in his ears, he shared his thoughts with the eager members who had come together for a communal washing and gathering of water.

Tautog began, his voice filled with a sense of purpose, "Brothers and sisters, our land has much to offer, and I believe we can find new ways to thrive and prosper. The changing season, the warmer weather, it brings with its opportunities for us to grow and build upon the knowledge we've gained."

He looked out at the natural surroundings, the forest's edge and the fields of potential. "Our ancestors were wise, and they taught us to live in harmony with the land. I propose that we expand our agricultural efforts, perhaps create new fields near the waterside. We can grow crops to sustain us throughout the year, and even trade with the Pilgrims."

A murmur of agreement swept through the gathered tribe members. Tautog's ideas were met with enthusiasm and a shared sense of hope. He was motivated by learning a new trade outside of fishing. Agriculture would be a new frontier to explore and master. He was ready for the challenge.

One of the elders, Wise Owl, spoke up, "Tautog, your thoughts are wise. We should also consider building more secure shelters. A strong village is built on strong foundations. With the knowledge of the Pilgrims and our own craftsmanship, we can create structures that will withstand the test of time. Perhaps we can line up the animals so feeding them becomes more efficient."

Others chimed in, offering their own insights and suggestions. Some spoke of exploring new hunting techniques, while others suggested trading and collaboration with neighboring tribes. The exchange of ideas flowed like the stream before them, connecting their thoughts and desires.

Tautog nodded, his heart brimming with pride in his people. "Let us not forget our traditions and our connection to the spirits of the land. As we embrace these new ideas, let us do so with respect for our heritage and the wisdom of our ancestors. We are a strong, resilient tribe, and together, we can create a better future."

With the promise of change and growth, the tribe's conversations continued, weaving dreams and possibilities into the fabric of their shared journey. In the heart of the stream's flowing waters, they found inspiration, and in the unity of their voices, they found the strength to explore new horizons.

Tautog, the vision of strength and wisdom, wrapped the yucca fabric around him and dried off after his cleansing in the stream. His hair, dark as the night sky, clung to his handsome face like glistening tendrils. As he shook his head from side to side, the droplets of water scattered like tiny jewels, and his mane came to life, captivating the tribal women who had gathered around.

With a humble and gracious smile, Tautog allowed the women to fuss over him, their admiration like a gentle caress. Their eyes sparkled with respect and affection, their hearts touched by the ideas he had shared.

As the tribal women offered their insights and support, Tautog nodded appreciatively. He understood the importance of their involvement, for it was the collective wisdom of their people that would shape their future. The men looked a bit envious at Tautog, but he would not be deterred. With a promise to consider their suggestions and share them with the Chief upon his return to camp, Tautog demonstrated his commitment to unity and progress.

In the heart of that moment, at the edge of the stream, their collective hopes and dreams painted a future ripe with possibilities. Tautog, the symbol of leadership and the embodiment of the tribe's spirit, stood as an executive of strength and potential of their people, ready to embark on the journey toward a brighter tomorrow.

As Tautog made his way back to the tribe's camp, he weaved through the playful chaos that unfolded near the cornfield. The laughter of children and the joyous shouts of boys and girls learning the art of archery filled the air. It was a scene that spoke of tradition and the passing of knowledge from one generation to the next.

The young ones, their faces illuminated with excitement, gathered around their elders. Each child held a bow with determined intent, their tiny hands gripping the wooden weapon. With arrows in hand, they listened to the guidance of the experienced hunters, whose wisdom and skill they aspired to inherit.

As the tribal elders shared their expertise, the children eagerly mimicked their movements, practicing the fine art of archery. They adjusted their stances, drew back the bows with earnest concentration, and aimed at imaginary prey with vivid imagination.

The adults watched with pride, offering encouragement and occasional laughter as arrows sometimes veered off course or missed their intended marks. The joy of discovery and the shared knowledge between generations wove a pattern of unity in the heart of the tribe.

The children's laughter was like music, their enthusiasm a gentle reminder to the tribe's enduring traditions. The lessons of the hunt and the passing down of skills were not only practical but also a reflection of the tribe's strong sense of community and their connection to the land.

As Tautog observed this scene, he couldn't help but feel a sense of optimism for the future. The playful learning of the young ones would ensure that the wisdom of their ancestors continued to thrive, as they embarked on their own journeys of growth, understanding, and shared vision within the tribe's camp.

As Tautog contemplated the notion of being a father, he couldn't help but be inundated by memories of his own father, Meta. The recollections were brief but intense, and they stirred within him a profound sense of loss and longing. His father's teachings and presence had been an anchor in his life, a guiding force that shaped his understanding of the world.

Observing John's role as a father to Silvia had left a lasting impression on Tautog. He recognized the love, support, and guidance that John offered to his daughter, and it filled him with a sense of admiration and wonder. The lessons of life, the tenderness of their relationship, and the way John nurtured Silvia's growth were qualities that Tautog aspired to embody.

However, Tautog also grappled with the question of how to learn from John without becoming a burden or intruding on their close-knit family bond. He didn't want to impose himself on their lives, but he yearned to absorb the wisdom and values that John exemplified.

With a deep breath, Tautog resolved to find a way to learn from John and to contribute to the shared wisdom between their cultures. As Tautog moved through the camp, he passed by a group of young girls engrossed in the art of crafting and decorating clay pots. Their nimble fingers shaped the clay with intricate patterns, their eyes filled with wonder and curiosity. Their dedication to this ancient skill refreshing.

As he observed their work, Tautog's thoughts turned to the future, and the idea of one day teaching his own son life lessons that he had gathered from his own experiences and the wisdom of his people. In the heart of his reflections, he noticed other men watching him and smiling. Some were jeering, some were hiding a laugh, but most were admiring him.

The village, under the guidance of Massasoit, thrived and prospered. The wisdom and leadership of their Chief was a true inspiration. Tautog felt a renewed vigor as he headed to his post as a fisherman, eager to cast off the weight of the past three years.

The memories of misunderstandings and confrontations with the Pilgrims still lingered, but Tautog was determined to focus on the brighter path ahead. As he prepared his fishing gear and ventured out into the waters, he left behind the trials and tribulations, embracing the future with hope and resilience.

In the heart of the river, with the gentle flow of the current, Tautog found solace and purpose. The fish were abundant, and their capture was a reminder of the sustenance that the land provided. Tautog's skills as a fisherman had been honed over the years, and he cast his nets with the expertise of generations.

As he hauled in the day's catch, he felt a deep sense of fulfillment and a renewed connection to the land, a connection that bridged the gap between his people and the Pilgrims. He was grounded and at peace. It was then that he thought of Silvia. He wanted to make a lasting impression on her, and his mind was at work thinking of ways to get her attention. She was of age to marry, and he didn't want to have any regrets.

With the bounty of the river in his nets and the memories of the past behind him, Tautog returned to the camp with a heart full of gratitude and determination. The lessons of the past were not forgotten, but they served as a foundation for a future built on understanding, cooperation, and the enduring spirit of their people.

As the sun dipped below the horizon, casting a warm, golden hue over the landscape, Tautog and Squanto joined John on the front porch of his cabin. Their day of fishing had been successful, and the camaraderie between the three of them was as strong as ever. The elder men could tell Tautog was still eager to see Silvia. With the gentle breeze rustling through the trees, they embarked on a new experience - learning how to smoke tobacco.

John had introduced the concept of smoking as a way to relax and unwind, explaining that it could have calming effects on the mind and spirit. Tautog knew the present-day effects of smoking, which he was sure John was not privy to. He listened anyway, enjoying the company. John carefully demonstrated the process, showing them how to pack the tobacco into a pipe and how to draw gently to release the fragrant smoke.

As they puffed on their pipes, Tautog and Squanto followed John's lead, inhaling the aromatic tendrils of tobacco. The experience was new to them, and they watched with curiosity as the smoke swirled and danced in the air. John explained that, when used in moderation, smoking could be a way to ease the mind and provide moments of relaxation. Tuatog in no way encouraged his fellow man to become addicted to smoking, so he made a mental note to speak to them about it back at camp. He smiled to himself knowing the importance of this knowledge, and with pride knowing that he was doing the responsible task of educating his tribe. John looked at Tautog smile, and felt a calming relief wash over him. He filled up his pipe and continued to cope with life's punishments.

Sitting on the porch steps, Silvia joined them with a tray of herbal teas in hand. The herbal concoctions were a blend of native plants and traditional English herbs, chosen for their soothing and calming properties. Silvia served the warm teas in earthenware cups, the fragrant steam rising to greet them. She did not let on that secretly she had been terrified of Tautog. She was hesitant to meet any of the Native Americans, and she felt propelled forward in their friendship by her father. Her mother's spirit, an invisible guiding force leading her into womanhood. She served these men out of a great respect and fear of the Lord.

As they sipped the teas and smoked their pipes, the conversation turned to the upcoming harvest. They discussed the crops, the potential yield, and the preparations needed for the changing seasons. Tautog shared the ideas from his tribe about expanding agricultural efforts, and Squanto spoke of the farming techniques he had learned in Europe.

In the heart of the gathering, there was a sense of unity and shared knowledge. The blending of cultures and traditions was evident in the fragrant smoke, the comforting warmth of herbal tea, and the exchange of ideas that promised a bountiful harvest. Silvia's presence, as always, was a bridge between their worlds, and the porch of John's cabin became a place of camaraderie and understanding in the heart of the New World.

Standing at the edge of the vast and magnificent fields, the party gazed over the thriving landscape that had been three years in the making.

The wheat fields stretched out like a golden sea, the rows of corn stood tall and proud, and the vibrant pumpkin patches promised a bountiful harvest. It was in itself a gospel of the Lord. No one had ever seen this vision of God's grace and love before. They found themselves in awe and wonderment to God's glory.

With the harvest season approaching in the next three months, they had meticulously planned their efforts to ensure a successful and prosperous yield. Their discussions included how they would closely monitor the growth of the crops, ensuring that they received adequate water and attention. Pests and weeds would be managed to protect the health of the plants. How they would store the crops, sell the crops, and share the crops.

All problems of the world seemed to roll off their shoulders when they discussed the planning together. They all laughed and enjoyed the labor, and loved even more so the freedom it gave them from the outside world. The tobacco was really taking hold over the men, and they felt relaxed and at ease. As the night was almost over, Squanto shared a bit about his kidnapping. He rarely every did, so everyone listened closely.

"I found myself in an unimaginable situation, one that shook the very core of my existence. Kidnapped, a world that seemed foreign and cruel, had become my reality." He looked down and acted as though he was confused.

"But now, in an unforeseen twist of fate, I had been seized, taken captive once more. The hands that had welcomed me back to these shores were now the same ones that held me against my will." He had a sense of helplessness in his voice. His story summed up the idea that even in a person's most content and confident moments, life could still be taken. Squanto's story reminded the party to remain steadfast, humble, together, and grateful in their journey.

After the weighty moment of silence that followed their discussion, the men rose to their feet, a sense of purpose in their stride. Tautog's embrace with Silvia was one of deep friendship and understanding, a connection that transcended the boundaries of culture and tradition.

As they bid their farewells, the older men, their shoulders bearing the weight of years of experience, couldn't help but feel a surge of youthful energy wash over them. In the presence of Tautog and Silvia, they had been reminded of the enduring power of unity, cooperation, and the boundless potential for growth and change.

For the next three months, the people of Plymouth worked tirelessly, their days stretching from the first light of dawn to the golden hues of sunset. From sun up to sun down, they toiled in the fields, tending to the crops that promised comfort for the coming Winter. There was little time for rest, as the promise of the bountiful harvest urged them forward.

Short breaks allowed them precious moments to catch their breath, to share laughter and stories with their loved ones under the warm sun. These fleeting respites were a reminder of the importance of community and the bonds that strengthened with every passing day.

As the day gave way to night, the harvest moon rose in the clear sky, its silvery glow casting a serene and guiding light over the land. In its gentle illumination, the people found solace and renewed determination, ready to embrace the next dew-filled day.

During this time, Silvia noticed an absence of her friend's presence. Tautog's time was spent at his camp and in the fields most days. The fishermen had been called to harvest the crops this time of year.

What Silvia did not know was that Tautog's tribe was bringing him home. Tautog found himself busied and gently pressured by the women of his tribe, who had a keen interest in seeing him settle down with a woman and begin the journey of building a family. Their persistent encouragement was rooted in the deep-seated desire to continue the tribe's legacy and maintain the bonds of their people.

The women kept Tautog engaged in various activities around the camp, recognizing that their skills and wisdom were vital for the well-being and sustainability of the tribe. Additionally, the women directed Tautog's attention to the upkeep and repair of the camp's fences, an essential aspect of safeguarding their community and resources. Tautog, strong and capable, embraced these responsibilities with dedication, understanding that their success was intertwined with the strength and cohesiveness of the tribe.

As the days passed, Tautog began to feel the weight of their expectations, mingled with a growing awareness of his role in the future of their people. The gentle insistence of the women, their guidance, and their nurturing presence served as a reminder of the importance of family and community in the life of the tribe.

While Tautog cherished his independence and the bonds he had formed with the Pilgrims, he knew that the legacy of his people rested on his shoulders, and the decision to build a family would shape the course of their future. The harmonious blend of tradition and change, like the intricate weaving of a basket, was solidifying his future.

In the stillness of the night, Silvia lay awake, the gentle embrace of moonlight spilling through the cabin's window. Her thoughts danced like fireflies in the darkness, and her heart carried the weight of a realization that had slowly taken root within her.

She missed the nightly talks with Tautog, the warmth of his presence by the fireside, and the wisdom that flowed from his words like a soothing melody. Their conversations had been a guiding light in her time in the New World, illuminating the path toward understanding and harmony. She knew the colony was criticizing her father for allowing her to spend so much time with this Native man. She did not want to let anyone down, and she also knew she had to follow her heart.

As she lay in her soft bed, her mind drifted to Tautog's rugged features, the strength in his gaze, and the kindness that resonated in his every smile. She realized that the connection they shared had transcended friendship, and in the quiet hours of the night, she acknowledged the depth of her feelings. The other Pilgrim boys appeared so fragile compared to Tautog. They seemed childish and petty. Tautog's calloused hands, sun-kissed skin, and belly laughs rolled through her mind.

A gentle flutter in her chest, like a bird's wing against her heart, revealed the truth. Silvia had come to romantically love Tautog, and the realization filled her with a sense of longing and yearning. She understood that the boundaries of culture and tradition could not extinguish the flame that had ignited within her.

Silvia's heart, like a compass, had found its direction, pointing her toward a future where understanding, unity, and the warmth of love could coexist, much like the harmony that had been cultivated in their shared journey through the New World.

In the heart of a world unknown and wild, a love did bloom, a story reconciled. Silvia, fair and with an open heart, found love transcending worlds, a work of art. In Tautog's rugged strength, she found her guide, a bridge between two worlds, none could divide. His wisdom, like a river flowing free, in Silvia's heart, it found its harmony.

As nights turned into days, a love took flight, their friendship blossomed into something more, a love, a longing, they could not ignore.

With every smile, a thousand stories told, in their shared moments, precious as pure gold. Silvia's love for Tautog, a gentle flame, A testament to love's unending aim. In unity, they found their shared domain, love's fire burned, regardless of the pain. Their love, an infinite construct became solid matter in the world, sorrow it would abduct, a love story engraved in the human heart. in the New World's embrace, their love unfurled, a resounding promise of love transcending the world.

As the last days of the harvest season drew to a close, the Pilgrims and Natives gathered together, their faces ripe with the satisfaction of a fruitful year. The idea of celebrating their shared abundance with a grand feast took root in their hearts, a gesture of gratitude for the blessings of their combined efforts. It was to be a three-day celebration of unity and thanksgiving.

Silvia, with her heart full of warmth and a determination to contribute to the festivities, took on the task of baking ten pumpkin pies. In her cozy home, the aroma of fresh pumpkin and spices filled the air, as she lovingly prepared each pie with skill and care.

Her fingers worked deftly, expertly mixing the pumpkin with the spices, and the sweet scent of cinnamon and nutmeg wafted through the cabin. Silvia's commitment to creating delicious pies to feed the hundreds of people in attendance reflected her appreciation for the friendship and community she had found in the New World. She had the pies lined up underneath the kitchen window. Silently, she prayed a small prayer of thanks for not owning any cats or dogs. The pie crusts were fresh and flaky, waiting for her to fill them. The crafted spiced and sweet pumpkin filling went in next. With a methodical approach, she slowly and carefully filled each crust to the top.

As the pies baked in the warmth of the hearth, Silvia couldn't help but smile, imagining the joy and togetherness that the upcoming celebration would bring. Her pies, each a labor of love, were a small but meaningful contribution to the Thanksgiving feast. Once they were baked and cooled, she added a dollop of whipped cream to each pie's center. She stored them in the cellar until the next day.

Thanksgiving arrived with a sense of anticipation and imagery, and the celebration was a sight to behold. Tables were erected at the end of the cornfield. Men had cut mazes into the fields for the children to enjoy while the women prepared for the feast. The tables were set with great care, covered with woven tablecloths and adorned with wildflowers and autumn leaves, creating a picturesque scene that celebrated the beauty of the New World. Candles were lit while plates and plates of food were situated in aesthetically appealing ways upon the top of each table.

It looked as though they were in a golden ballroom, only they were outdoors and chairs were placed closely together on either side of every table. The gathering was a diverse mixture of people, a coming together of different cultures in a spirit of gratitude. Native Americans, their vibrant clothing and traditional regalia a vivid display of their heritage, mingled with Pilgrims dressed in simple yet elegant garments. The Pilgrim's went to extremes to dye their clothes black to show reverence and respect for their guests.

The Pilgrims brought their finest gifts including mashed potatoes and gravy. At the center of the feast, perfectly roasted turkeys, gifts from the Native Americans, took pride of place. They were seasoned with native herbs and spices, a symbol of cooperation and shared abundance.

The Pilgrim women had fun and experimented with different dishes. They brought stuffing. It was fragrant, herb-infused stuffing made from local grains, herbs, and vegetables. Creamy mashed potatoes flanked the turkeys, a comfort food, garnished with butter and chives.

Homemade cranberry sauce, a sweet-tart addition that added a burst of color to the table was added in boats surrounding the stuffing. Finally, a variety of freshly baked bread, including cornbread and wheat rolls, symbolizing the fusion of old and new world ingredients.

The tribe, too, experimented with different dishes. They brought succotash- a savory dish made from lima beans and corn, a staple of the Native American diet. They made a Three Sisters Salad- A salad of beans, corn, and squash. Succulent, roasted venison was presented, seasoned with indigenous spices, showcasing the hunting skills of the Native Americans. Freshly caught fish from the local streams, a reflection of their expertise in fishing also made the table. Finally, cornbread- unleavened and hearty.

Amid the abundance of food, discussions around the table were heartfelt and meaningful. People shared their stories, spoke of gratitude for the past year's harvest, and reflected on the journey of understanding and cooperation that had brought them to this moment. The discussions were centered around their families, their upbringings, and shared skills and talents. Each family did their best to stay open-minded and peaceful.

Thanksgiving was not only a feast for the body but also a feast for the soul, a celebration of shared humanity, and the enduring spirit of collaboration that had brought two cultures together in harmony.

Silvia's heart raced as she found herself in the presence of Tautog, the man who had captured her affections. The watchful eyes of the other women in the tribe did not go unnoticed, and she couldn't help but feel self-conscious under their scrutinizing gaze. They, too, wondered whether Tautog would take any steps to acknowledge their deepening connection.

Amid the celebration, the air was thick with anticipation, and Silvia's emotions ran deep. She was torn between the longing in her heart and the awareness of the cultural differences that stood between them. Silvia knew that the road to understanding and acceptance was a challenging one, but her feelings for Tautog were undeniable.

As the feast continued, there were shared smiles and exchanged glances, hinting at a connection that transcended spoken words. Silvia's heart fluttered with hope and desire, wondering if this Thanksgiving would be the moment when their unspoken feelings would find expression. The uncharted territory of their evolving relationship was both thrilling and filled with uncertainty, a reflection of the complex dance of emotions between two people from different worlds.

As the feast came to an end, and the last remnants of a bountiful meal were cleared away, Tautog took Silvia by the hand, surprising her and the onlookers. They ventured to the edge of the forest, where the world seemed to be bathed in the soft, golden light of the setting sun. There, under the embrace of ancient trees and the gentle rustling of leaves, Tautog took a deep breath and reached for his Harvest Talisman.

With a voice filled with emotion, he began to tell Silvia an incredible story, one that transcended the boundaries of time and space. He recounted his journey from a distant future, a time long after her own, and the trials and challenges that had brought him to this moment in the New World.

Silvia listened with rapt attention, her heart both astonished and moved by the depth of Tautog's story. As he shared his journey, the tears welled up in his eyes, and he held onto her as the weight of his experiences washed over him. Silvia, taken aback by this raw vulnerability, wrapped her arms around him, offering her silent support and understanding.

In that sacred moment at the forest's edge, their worlds intertwined, and their connection deepened. Silvia realized that the love she felt for Tautog went beyond the boundaries of time and cultural differences, she found herself a part of a story that was both extraordinary and deeply human.

Silvia's heart swelled with emotion as Tautog told her the legend of the Harvest Talisman. He told her he believed she was the one he came back for. He asked for her assistance in burying the Harvest Talisman, with its precious seed at its center, right there in the forest. Without hesitation, she knelt down beside him, feeling the earth beneath her fingers and the connection that bound them to the land. Her chest heaved at the gravity of the moment, and she found it difficult to believe that he thought of her with such magnitude and duty.

Together, they carefully buried the talisman, placing it deep within the soil, where it would become one with the earth. Tautog's words resonated in the quiet of that moment, and Silvia could sense the significance of their act. The seed at the center symbolized their shared bond, a testament to their love and the hope for a future that would continue to grow and flourish, just as the seed would sprout in the rich soil.

As they stood there, hand in hand, the forest played witness to their unique love story. The otherworldliness of this act showed itself moments later. As they were still enjoying the moment of togetherness, a small sapling sprouted from the very spot in which they had just buried the talisman, proving that some force beyond their control had brought them together.

In the shadows, Mahkah also witnessed this miracle. She was the one whom the angel had visited in the first place, and she was also the one who welcomed Tautog from the future. Realization hit her in this moment that something radical had to have happened and life had to have continued on far past her own years for Tautog to have received the talisman in the future to begin with. She felt a sense of security and peace as she left the two lovers in privacy.

Chapter Five- Bonded Trusts

AMIDST THE CAMP'S BUSTLING activity and the flickering glow of the campfire, Tautog sought a moment of solitude with Squanto. The two men, each with a history of their own, found a quiet corner where they could converse away from prying eyes and curious ears.

Tautog, his eyes filled with a mixture of longing and determination, turned to Squanto, a trusted friend who had walked a similar path of understanding and unity. With the crackling fire as their only witness, he began to speak of his love for Silvia.

"Squanto," Tautog began, "I have found a love that transcends the boundaries of our worlds. Silvia, the Pilgrim woman, has captured my heart, and in her, I see a future we could build together." Squanto, wise and understanding, listened attentively, recognizing the depth of Tautog's feelings. He knew that love was a force that could bridge the gaps between people, just as their shared experiences had done.

Tautog continued, "She is like the sweetest berry on the bush, and her spirit shines like the sun. I believe that our love can be a symbol of unity and hope for our people, for the future we dream of." Squanto, with hope, placed a reassuring hand on Tautog's shoulder. "Love knows no boundaries, my friend," he replied. "If your heart has found its home with Silvia, then follow it.

With Squanto's support and the shared vision of a brighter future, Tautog's love for Silvia found validation and a sense of purpose. In the quiet of their camp, beneath the starry skies of the New World, he knew he had the tribe's support. Squanto encouraged Tautog to go to bed and think about why he loved Silvia and to act on his feelings.

As Tautog lay in his simple cot, the soft rustling of the camp's night sounds enveloped him. His mind was awash with a turbulent sea of thoughts, a cascade of emotions that left him wrestling with uncertainty and doubt. Squanto's words of wisdom echoed in his mind as he contemplated the barriers that stood between him and his love for Silvia.

In the stillness of the night, Tautog's inner monologue unfolded:

"Could my love for Silvia ever be enough to bridge the gap between us? Is it possible that John, her father, harbors suspicions about me, my origins, and my intentions? The tale of time-travel I shared with Silvia could be a source of doubt, a reason for skepticism.

John, the Pilgrim who has welcomed me into his home and heart, may now question the depths of my honesty and the authenticity of my intentions. I can't blame him; what I've shared is beyond the ordinary, beyond belief. He seems just forward-thinking enough to fathom that I am telling the truth. He has been so good to my people without even knowing them.

Silvia, a vision of warmth and understanding, has shown me a world of love and unity. But the fear of misunderstanding, of breaking the trust that has been built, is a weight that lies heavy on my heart. The duty I am beginning to feel for her is like a steep cliff that I will soon fall over. Love, as powerful as it may be, could be a fickle friend.

. I must find a way to navigate this delicate terrain, to prove my sincerity, and to earn the trust of those who have welcomed me into their world. Sleep, however elusive it may be tonight, brings with it the promise of a new day. A day where I can face these challenges head-on, where love, understanding, and the hope for unity guide my path forward."

With these thoughts swirling in his mind, Tautog sought rest beneath the moonlit sky, hopeful that the dawn would bring clarity and the strength to overcome the obstacles that lay ahead.

Tautog made his way to John's cabin. In his hands, he carried a bundle of handmade cards, each one adorned with colorful drawings created by the camp's children. Turkeys, corn, and happy people were lovingly illustrated, capturing the spirit of the upcoming Thanksgiving celebration.

Bright and early, Tautog approached the cabin, his heart filled with a mixture of anticipation and hope. He had been reflecting on Squanto's wisdom and his own inner monologue from the previous night, determined to find a way to strengthen the bonds of trust and understanding.

With a soft knock at the door, Tautog waited for John to answer. When the door swung open, Tautog greeted him with a warm smile and extended the bundle of cards toward John.

"These are cards created by the children of our camp," Tautog explained. "They've drawn pictures of turkeys, corn, and joy, in celebration of the Thanksgiving feast we will all share. We hope you'll find them as heartwarming as we do."

Tautog's gesture reflected his desire to extend an olive branch, a reminder that they were all part of a larger family in the New World. With the spirit of Thanksgiving in the air, he hoped that this simple act of kindness would help mend any doubts and reinforce the bonds of trust that had been forming as thick as the thatched roof he was under.

As the door to John's cabin swung open, revealing Silvia deep in her needlepointing, she was startled by Tautog's arrival. Her work fell from her hands, forgotten in an instant as she rushed to greet him with a warm and embracing hug.

The sight of Silvia's spontaneous embrace filled the room with warmth and emotion. John, standing beside them, could not help but smile at the genuine affection between his daughter and Tautog. It was evident that the gratitude he felt for Tautog was sincere and profound.

The unspoken understanding between the three of them, the silent recognition of Tautog's role in their lives, permeated the air. In that moment, as they stood together in John's cabin, their hearts were connected by a shared appreciation for the journey they had embarked upon and the love that had taken root in their hearts.

Throughout the day, as they reveled in the sense of accomplishment that surrounded them, John, Tautog, and Silvia also dedicated time to discussing their upcoming winter plans. The New World's changing seasons demanded careful preparation, and together they crafted a detailed plan for the cold months ahead.

They decided to reinforce their cabins and add extra insulation to make them as cozy and warm as possible. They would gather firewood in abundance to ensure a steady supply of heat during the colder days and nights.

A large portion of their discussions revolved around food storage. They knew that the harsh winter could make hunting and foraging difficult. So, they planned to dry and preserve surplus fruits and vegetables for the winter months, while also setting up an area to store dried meats, salted fish, and grains.

They agreed that the harsh winters would be more bearable if they continued to share meals together, creating a sense of unity and warmth during the coldest of days. Recognizing the importance of community support, they planned to share resources, tools, and knowledge to ensure that everyone in the camp had what they needed to weather the winter months. They'd hold regular gatherings to exchange ideas and make sure everyone was prepared.

Winter would also be a time for continued learning. John, Silvia, and Tautog saw it as an opportunity to further their understanding of each other's cultures and strengthen the bonds between the Pilgrims and the Native Americans.

As they sat together, discussing their winter plans and the challenges that lay ahead, Tautog could no longer contain the depth of his feelings for Silvia. The words of love he had harbored in his heart welled up, and he felt compelled to share them with John, the man who had welcomed him into his home.

Tautog interrupted John's planning, his voice trembling with emotion but filled with sincerity. "John," he began, "there's something I need to tell you, and it's a matter of the heart." John, surprised by the interruption, turned his attention to Tautog, his brow furrowing in curiosity. "Of course, Tautog. What's on your mind?"

With a deep breath, Tautog continued, his gaze never leaving John's. "I have come to deeply care for your daughter, Silvia. The love that has blossomed between us is something I can no longer keep hidden. It transcends the differences of our worlds, and it is a love that I hold in the highest regard."

John listened, his expression a mix of surprise, understanding, and appreciation for Tautog's honesty. He recognized the strength of Tautog's feelings and the importance of their shared bond. Tautog continued, "I would like your blessing to seek Silvia's hand in marriage, not just as a gesture of love but as a symbol of unity between our people."

John, taking a moment to absorb Tautog's words, finally smiled. "Tautog, your honesty and your willingness to bridge the gaps between our worlds mean a great deal to me. I can see the sincerity in your eyes, and I believe that love knows no boundaries. If Silvia's heart is as open to this union as yours, then I would be honored to give my blessing."

The weight of unspoken doubts lifted, replaced by understanding and respect.

John's face was frozen in curiosity and a touch of perplexity as he considered the implications of Tautog's heartfelt confession. He knew that Tautog's love for Silvia was genuine, but he had important questions that needed answers. With a deep breath, he decided to inquire further.

"Tautog," John began, "your love for Silvia is evident, and your intentions are sincere. But I have to ask, are you planning on staying in the colony, or do you have other plans?"

Tautog met John's gaze with honesty and openness. "John, I've found a place in my heart for this world, for the people I've come to know and care for. But I must also tell you the truth about my origins. I come from a time that is not this time, a future that is not this future."

John's brow furrowed as he processed Tautog's words. "You mean to say that you come from a different time, a different world?" Tautog nodded solemnly. "Yes, that's correct. Silvia knows about my time-traveling journey, and it's a part of our shared history. The love we've found is deep and genuine, but it's complicated by the fact that we may need to return to the future at some point."

John's perplexity deepened, but he appreciated Tautog's honesty. "I see. This is indeed a complex situation. I respect your honesty, Tautog, and I also understand that love knows no boundaries. Silvia's happiness is important to me, and I believe in your love for her. But we'll have to navigate this together, with open hearts and a shared understanding of the challenges that lie ahead." John wondered what the other members of Plymouth would think if he allowed Silvia to run away with Tautog to some foreign place.

Tautog nodded, a sense of relief washing over him that he had been able to share his truth with John. As John contemplated the implications of Tautog's revelation, he realized that their situation was not without its challenges. The prospect of a time-traveler from the future raising complex questions about the peace they had found in these years. Uncertainty hung in the air, and John decided to voice his concerns, seeking clarity and understanding.

"Tautog," John began, "I've been thinking about what your presence here and your relationship with Silvia mean for the future. We've worked hard to find peace and unity in this New World, but we must also be prepared for the uncertainties that lie ahead. What does the future hold for Silvia if she chooses to stay with you?"

Tautog met John's gaze with a sense of responsibility. "I understand your concerns, John. Silvia and I have discussed this at length. If we choose to return to the future, she would be leaving behind everything she's known. But the love we share and the bond we've built are strong, and we believe that the future can hold new opportunities for both of us."

John's eyes reflected his fatherly concern. "And what about the peace we've found here? Will your presence and your knowledge of the future disrupt that?"

Tautog's response was measured and thoughtful. "I would never want to disrupt the peace or unity we've found. In fact, I hope that my presence and the knowledge I bring can be a source of strength. I want to work with our community to preserve what we've achieved and to face the future together, gracefully."

John nodded, his concern not completely dissipated but his trust in Tautog's intentions evident. "Your honesty and your commitment to our community are important to me. We will need to navigate these challenges together, with open hearts and a shared vision for the future."

As their conversation continued, it was clear that Tautog and John were committed to finding a path forward that balanced their love for Silvia, and they knew just how to do it. Silvia was a confident woman at this point, and she knew she wanted to marry Tautog as well.

John's primary concern was his daughter, Silvia, and her happiness. After a thoughtful consideration of the situation and a deep understanding of Tautog's love for her, he made a heartfelt decision. With a sense of determination and genuine affection for both of them, John addressed Tautog.

"Tautog," he said, "Silvia's future and her happiness are what matter most to me. I can see the love you share, and I can see the unity you represent. If you wish to ask Silvia to marry you, I want you to know that I support your decision wholeheartedly. If she says yes, she will have my full support, and we will navigate this journey together as a family."

Tautog, deeply moved by John's words and the sincerity in his eyes, nodded with gratitude. "Thank you, John. Your understanding and support mean the world to me. I promise to cherish Silvia and do my best to make her happy."

. John's decision to support Tautog's proposal was a signal to the power of love and the unbreakable bonds that had been forged in the New World. Together, they would face the challenges and joys of the journey ahead, hand in hand.

With John's blessing and the newfound sense of purpose, Tautog left John's cabin with a renewed sense of determination and invigoration. He made his way to the stream where he had first met Silvia, the place that held the memories of their initial encounter.

Beside the babbling waters of the stream, he knelt in prayer, seeking guidance and clarity. The gentle rustling of leaves and the soft trickle of the stream seemed to whisper secrets of the heart. Tautog bowed his head in quiet communion with the divine.

As he prayed, Tautog felt a sense of guidance and purpose washing over him. It was as if a voice from within, a divine presence, whispered to his heart, offering a path forward. In the stillness of the natural world, he heard a clear message.

God told him to propose to Silvia in front of the ancient tree, the very spot where the Harvest Talisman was buried. It was a sacred place that held the power of their shared history, a place where their love had taken root. It felt like a message from above, a call to celebrate their unity and to honor the journey that had brought them together.

Filled with a profound sense of destiny, Tautog knew that the time had come to take this monumental step in their love story. With his heart uplifted and his spirits soaring, he set off toward the tree, where he would soon ask Silvia for her hand in marriage, sealing their love of a bright future.

In a world of uncertainty, where futures collide, A father's love tested, emotions set to ride. For Silvia, his daughter, a bloom of pure grace, John faced a decision, a path to embrace. A month's passing brought changes untold, as love's pictured weaved, its threads pure gold. But John's heart was heavy, his thoughts deep and wide, as he contemplated, in shadows, he'd confide.

His love for his daughter, a bond ever true, he'd nurtured, protected, as fathers will do. But the time had now come, a letting goes, so bittersweet, to honor her love, their destiny to meet. With courage and grace, he embraced the unknown, the journey before them, a seed they had sown. For love knows no borders, no bounds to contain, in the tapestry of life, new threads to obtain.

Silvia, his daughter, her heart led the way, in the warmth of her smile, he found solace each day. Their love would endure, as it always had been, a father's farewell, with pride in his grin.

A new chapter dawning, with love's tender care, Silvia would journey, a future to share. As the winds of change blew, their spirits aglow, John's heart found its strength in letting her go.

As Winter's embrace settled over the land, Tautog prepared for a momentous day. Wrapped in layers of warm attire to ward off the chill, he set out to pick up Silvia. With each step, his excitement grew, and his heart raced with anticipation.

At Silvia's doorstep, Tautog arrived, his breath forming clouds in the crisp winter air. She emerged, adorned in her Winter attire, her cheeks flushed with the rosy hue of the season. With a warm smile, he offered her his hand, and they set off together, their journey filled with shared joy and a sense of contentment.

They ventured to the edge of the forest, where they had once buried the Harvest Talisman with a seed at its center. To their astonishment, the sapling that had sprouted from that sacred burial had flourished beyond their wildest expectations. What had once been a fragile sapling now stood as a magnificent oak tree, its branches stretching toward the heavens, its roots deeply intertwined with the earth.

Silvia gasped in awe, her eyes wide with wonder. Tautog, with a proud smile, gestured toward the towering oak. "Look, Silvia, at what our love has nurtured, a symbol of our unity and the strength of our bond."

Hand in hand, they stood beneath the grand oak tree, its branches swaying in the winter breeze. It had grown as strong and majestic as the tree that now stood before them. With their hearts intertwined like the roots of the oak and their love reaching skyward like its branches, Silvia and Tautog embraced. In the midst of the Winter's gentle snowfall, beneath the grand oak tree, so tall, Tautog knelt upon one knee, his heart's desire, Silvia, his love so free.

A ring fashioned from metal, pure and bright, a symbol of their love, a radiant light. in the pristine snow, so pure and cold, A story of love, forever to be told. With a trembling heart and a soul so bold, Tautog spoke, his words of love, he unrolled. "Silvia, my love, my heart's delight, in the quiet of Winter, with snow so white,

You've filled my life with love and grace, with every smile and tender embrace. Will you be mine, forevermore, in this world we've built, to explore? Like the snow that blankets this sacred ground, our love is pure, and in it, we're bound. Silvia, my dearest, in the Winter's embrace, will you marry me, and fill my days with grace?"

The snowflakes danced around them, light as air, As Silvia's eyes shone, her heart laid bare. With tears of joy and a radiant smile, she said, "Yes, my love, let's walk this mile."

Hand in hand, in the Winter's glow, beneath the oak tree, their love would grow. United in love, forever they'd be, in the heart of winter, for all to see. In that moment by the tree, a burning fire only they could see. An unfathomable force burned a heart into the trunk of the oak for eternity. The couple stood in awe, their mouths agape, watching their love seal their fate and escape.

Beneath the grand oak's ancient, towering crown, a force unseen, a power yet unknown. Silvia and Tautog, their love profound, lifted from the earth, their spirits overthrown. In an instant, through time they soared, as they left the past, together they adored. A journey through the ages, so swift and bold, their love's story was strong, like the tall rigid oak. He clung to her tightly, his treasure at last, they swirled and twirled in time's sweet dance.

Transcending time, like a whisper on the wind, Silvia and Tautog, their journey soon began. To a future unknown, a world to explore, their love's adventure, they now implore. In the year 2050, they did arrive, In Tautog's boat, RobEE, they reimagined. A world transformed, a future so bright, Together, they'd face the unknown, with all their might.

Hand in hand, their love, a beacon of light, Silvia and Tautog, their hearts taking flight. With each moment, they'd make history anew, a love that time could not subdue. In their wake, a great oak stood. With shoes of the couple resting at its feet. A tribe depleted of their leader, and a father ripped away from the love of his daughter. Fate had a way of taking what it wanted.

As they arrived in the year 2050, Tautog marveled at the world around him, the sights and sounds of a future he could barely fathom. But his attention soon turned to Silvia, who stood in the electric boat, her expression a mix of awe and sheer horror.

Tautog approached her with a gentle touch, a reassuring smile on his face. "Silvia, my love, I know this is overwhelming, but you are safe. We've traveled through time, and this boat is like nothing we've ever seen. It's powered by electricity, a force of the future." Silvia's eyes widened with a mix of confusion and fear. "Electricity? But how does it work, Tautog? This is so different from anything I've ever known."

Tautog took a deep breath, realizing the enormity of the situation. "Silvia, in the future, electricity is harnessed to power many things, just like the way the sun, wind, and water are used to generate energy. It's a cleaner, more sustainable source of power."

He continued to explain, "This boat, called RobEE, is an electric boat. It's powered by batteries that store electrical energy. It's much quieter and more environmentally friendly than the boats of our time. We're here to explore this world and learn, my love."

Silvia, though still anxious, began to absorb Tautog's words and felt a growing sense of trust. She took his hand and nodded. "I may not understand it all, Tautog, but as long as we're together, I'm ready to face this future with you."

Tautog smiled, his heart full of love and relief. Together, they would navigate this unknown world, hand in hand, with their love as their guiding light. Silvia clung to Tautog, her heart racing as the reality of their time-travel adventure settled in. The future was both fascinating and daunting, and the unfamiliar technology left her feeling overwhelmed. She needed a way to cope with the enormity of the moment.

As she held onto Tautog, her mind began to drift back to the Mayflower, the ship that had carried their ancestors to the New World. The memories of those early days, the struggles and triumphs of their forebears, provided her with a sense of resilience and determination.

Tautog, noticing the shift in her demeanor, held her even closer. "Silvia, I know this is a lot to take in, but we carry the strength and spirit of our ancestors within us. Just as they faced the unknown, we too can embrace the challenges of this new world, hand in hand."

Silvia nodded, her thoughts finding solace in the stories of those who had ventured into the unknown before them. With Tautog's reassuring presence and the resilience of their shared heritage, she began to acclimate to the future and to muster the courage to face whatever lay ahead.

Their love and the echoes of history would guide them as they navigated this unfamiliar landscape, forging their own path in a world that was yet to be explored. As Silvia began to acclimate to the world of 2050, she couldn't help but feel a sense of curiosity and wonder about what lay ahead. Turning to Tautog, she asked, "What will we do now, Tautog? How will we fit into this new world?"

Tautog, eager to provide her with some understanding and reassurance, began to share his knowledge of the time they had arrived in. He spoke about his family's business, their wealth, and the common facts about 2050, all while Silvia listened attentively, absorbing the information.

And then, with a warm smile, he said, "You know, Silvia, some things never change. Even in this future, Thanksgiving still exists. It's a time when people come together to give thanks for the blessings in their lives and share a meal with loved ones. It's a tradition that has endured, much like our love." He looked radiant and youthful as he boasted on this modern tradition.

Silvia's eyes brightened at the thought of spending more Thanksgivings with him, a cherished tradition that had been part of their shared history. She took Tautog's hand, her heart full of hope and anticipation for the future. "Tautog, as long as we're together, I believe we can find our place in this world, just as we've always done. Let's embrace this new adventure, hand in hand."

With their love as their guide and the knowledge of their shared history as their foundation, they were ready to embark on the journey of the future, knowing that some traditions, like Thanksgiving, would continue to remind them of the enduring power of togetherness and gratitude.

As Silvia discovered that the cherished tradition of Thanksgiving persisted in this new world, she felt a sense of empowerment and connection to her own history. It was a comforting reminder that some things transcended time and change, and the feast they had shared just one month ago held a special place in her heart.

Tautog, eager to show her the world of 2050, took her to a bustling mall where the modern conveniences of shopping and fashion were on full display. Silvia's eyes widened as she perused the aisles of designer dresses, each one more elegant and extravagant than the last.

With a sense of awe, she found herself trying on these exquisite garments, feeling like a modern-day princess in the vibrant colors and luxurious fabrics. The selection was overwhelming, and she couldn't help but be captivated by the fashion of the future.

As Silvia tried on dress after dress, she couldn't resist their allure. Tautog watched with a loving smile as she found herself drawn to the styles of this new world. With each dress she selected, she embraced the opportunity to become part of the 2050 culture, even if no one would believe her true origins as an authentic Pilgrim.

Her purchases added up to a sum that would have been unimaginable in her time, over $5000 on designer dresses. She felt a sense of transformation, embracing the beauty and modernity of this world, all while carrying the traditions and values of her Pilgrim heritage within her. She made sure to check the fabric of the garments she was purchasing. She found: High-Tech fabrics. These fabrics with advanced properties, such as self-cleaning, self-repairing, and adaptable to climate conditions, are popular in futuristic fashion. She bought 3D-printed clothing that was customizable, holographic material, and dresses that has bioluminescent accents. Each purchase made her wish her dad could see her now.

She was taken aback by the ease of purchasing these items as well as the ease of carrying them out of the mall in multi-colored bags. Almost everything about this world felt like a dream. No longer was she spending all of her time thinking about survival.

In this new world, Silvia may have been seen as a celebrity, a living relic from the past, but in her heart, she was simply a woman embracing the joys and opportunities of the future, all while honoring her rich history. With Tautog by her side, she was ready to write a new chapter in their love story, one that would span the ages. Hearing the people talk at the mall, she realized where Tautog's accent came from. She made a mental note to practice speaking in modern English.

Silvia, having indulged in the world of 2050's fashion and beauty, transformed herself into a vision of modern elegance. She carefully applied modern perfumes and makeup, enhancing her natural beauty and radiance. When she stepped out, she looked like a model straight off a fashion magazine cover.

Tautog, or rather, Philip, was taken aback by her stunning transformation. His heart swelled with pride and admiration as he gazed upon her, struck by her grace and the sheer luminosity of her presence. "Silvia," he said, his voice filled with awe, "you are the most beautiful woman in this world and the next. Your beauty shines as bright as your heart."

Silvia smiled, her eyes sparkling with newfound confidence. "Thank you, Philip. With your support and love, I'm ready to embrace this new world, just as I've embraced you and our incredible journey together. "Philip nodded, his heart bursting with love for the remarkable woman by his side.

As Philip and Silvia prepared to leave the bustling shopping district, Philip ushered her towards a sleek and silent vehicle, his Tesla. Its smooth lines and quiet electric engine stood in stark contrast to the horse-drawn carriages Silvia was accustomed to.

As they drove through the futuristic cityscape, Silvia's wonder and confusion coexisted, making her transition into this new world a delightful and sometimes bewildering experience. But with Philip's patient guidance, she was ready to embrace the possibilities of the future, one surprising moment at a time.

As Philip drove Silvia up to his mother's expansive estate, her eyes widened in amazement. The grandeur of the property and the magnificent mansion that loomed before her made her feel like royalty. She couldn't help but draw parallels to the grandeur of European royalty, yet as she had learned earlier, there was no longer a Queen of England.

Feeling a mix of apprehension and excitement, Silvia looked at Philip and said, "This estate is beyond anything I could have imagined, Philip. I feel like a queen, yet I understand there is no longer a queen in England. I must be prepared to meet your family, but I'm more than happy to go inside with you."

With his reassuring smile and hand in hers, Philip led Silvia through the grand entrance of the mansion, where they would soon encounter his family and begin a new chapter of their lives in this astonishing future. He loved the fact that their ancestral heritage was woven into time and that the product of their family's actions led to this luxury.

Weetamoo, Philip's mother, greeted her son with a warm embrace as they entered the grand mansion. It had only been a day in her time since they had celebrated Thanksgiving together, and she was delighted to see him again. Weetamoo was a woman of grace and poise, her regal presence echoing the elegance of the estate.

She looked at Philip and then at Silvia, who stood beside him, a radiant smile on her face. "Philip, who is this lovely lady?" Weetamoo inquired with a tone of curiosity. "Why didn't you bring her to our festivities last night?"

Philip, not wanting to reveal the truth about his riveting adventure, smiled warmly and replied, "Mother, this is Silvia, my fiancée. We thought it was time to introduce her properly to our family." Weetamoo's eyes sparkled with delight. "A fiancée? How splendid!" She turned to Silvia with a welcoming smile. "My dear, it's a pleasure to meet you. I'm Weetamoo, Philip's mother. Come, let me give you a tour of our home."

Weetamoo's graciousness and warmth put Silvia at ease as they embarked on a tour of the magnificent mansion. Silvia couldn't help but be enchanted by the opulence and history of the place, as well as the regal charm of her future mother-in-law. Little did she know that their journey through time had led them to a future filled with new experiences and extraordinary encounters.

Weetamoo's home was a sanctuary of opulence and refinement, a testament to the wealth and luxury of their time. As Silvia and Weetamoo embarked on the tour, the grandeur of the estate unfolded before Silvia's eyes. She felt a bit self-conscious, but when Weetamoo looked over at her as they walked, feelings in insecurity melted away.

Throughout the tour, Silvia marveled at the blend of classic and modern elements, as well as the attention to detail and craftsmanship that defined Weetamoo's home. The luxury and elegance of the estate were a testament to the wealth and sophistication of this future world, making Silvia's transition into this new life all the more extraordinary.

After their tour, Weetamoo graciously departed into the kitchen, extending an open invitation to Silvia to visit anytime she pleased.

Silvia was struck by Weetamoo's warmth and hospitality. She couldn't help but feel a growing sense of gratitude for the welcoming atmosphere in this magnificent home. Philip led Silvia to her new bedroom, which was indeed huge and awe-inspiring. The room was a sanctuary of modern luxury and comfort. Here are some of the details: The bedroom was incredibly spacious, with high ceilings and large windows that allowed natural light to flood the room. A king-sized bed with a plush, cloud-like mattress and soft linens dominated the room's center. The headboard was adorned with intricate woodwork. Finally, a walk-in closet that could easily be mistaken for a small boutique provided ample space for Silvia's clothing and belongings.

As Silvia settled into her new surroundings, a sense of dread began to build in the pit of her stomach. It was an inexplicable feeling, an unease she couldn't quite put her finger on. The splendor of the mansion and the warmth of Weetamoo and Philip's family contrasted sharply with the apprehension that was slowly gnawing at her. She couldn't help but wonder if it was a premonition of something yet unknown, a feeling that would challenge her newfound life in this mysterious future.

As Philip left her for a while to attend to other matters, Silvia found herself in her luxurious new bedroom, feeling a mixture of excitement and curiosity about her new life in this future world. Eager to learn and adapt, she decided to explore her surroundings and make herself at home.

Silvia's gaze fell upon a sleek, flat-screen television mounted on the wall. It was a baffling device to her, but she was determined to understand it. She tentatively pressed the power button on the remote control, and the screen came to life with a bright display of colors. She saw images and heard voices emanating from the screen, and she watched in wonder as a new form of entertainment unfolded before her eyes.

Silvia began the process of unpacking her belongings. She marveled at the ample closet space and hung her newly acquired modern dresses with care. The closet seemed to go on forever, and she couldn't help but smile at the thought of all the outfits she could explore.

Silvia placed her personal items on the nightstand, including a small wooden chest that contained her cherished trinkets and mementos from her time. It was a comforting reminder of her roots and the journey that had brought her here.

She couldn't resist the allure of the luxurious bedding and the softness of the pillows. Silvia reclined on the king-sized bed, feeling a sense of comfort and peace wash over her. The sense of dread that had lingered earlier began to fade as she settled into her new environment.

Silvia noticed a small bookshelf filled with a variety of books from different genres. She selected a novel and decided to start reading, eager to embrace this new world's literature.

As Silvia navigated this unfamiliar territory, her sense of adventure and willingness to adapt outweighed her earlier apprehension. The discovery of modern technology and the comforts of her new home filled her with a sense of wonder and intrigue, setting the stage for the next chapter of her journey in this mysterious future.

Philip's presence in her new bedroom brought Silvia a sense of comfort and security, and she had never felt more comfortable in her entire life. She marveled at the modern amenities, like the heated floors, that surrounded her in this grand room. The contrast with her previous life in the 17th century was striking.

As the day ended, Philip and Silvia knelt together by the bedside, holding hands in prayer. They both found solace in their shared faith and the familiar practice of seeking guidance from Jesus.

Philip planted a tender kiss on Silvia's cheek before leaving her to rest in her new surroundings. She lay in her opulent bed, feeling a sense of gratitude for this new life and a growing affection for Philip. With a heart full of hope and wonder, she drifted into a peaceful slumber, ready to embrace the mysteries of the future that lay ahead.

Philip's heart raced as he lay in bed, the lingering memories of the horrific experience he had just endured vivid in his mind. He couldn't shake the feeling of dread that had enveloped him, and he knew it was no mere nightmare; it had been all too real. What made it even more unsettling was the presence of Silvia beside him, who had shared in this strange and distressing event.

As he tried to make sense of what had happened, he couldn't help but feel an overwhelming sense of protectiveness and concern for Silvia, who had been at his side throughout it all. They had journeyed through time together, faced the unknown, and were now grappling with a reality neither of them could fully understand.

Philip's thoughts raced, and he knew that their future held more mysteries and challenges than he could have ever imagined. With Silvia by his side, he was determined to unravel the truth behind their extraordinary experiences and protect her from whatever dangers lay ahead.

Chapter Six- Escaping the Aftermath

IN THE DANCE OF TWO worlds, with cultures unknown, misunderstandings, like shadows, have grown. The Wampanoag's ways, steeped in ancient lore, clash with the expectations of those who stepped ashore.

The Europeans arrived with hopes and dreams anew, Their visions of the future, like morning's early dew. But the Wampanoag's customs, their rhythms and their rhyme, were seen as foreign mysteries in this uncharted time. The Europeans sought to till the land and build, their concepts of ownership, to the Wampanoag, seemed unfulfilled. They tilled and sowed, and built fences to mark, Their misunderstandings, like fissures in the dark.

The Wampanoag, stewards of the land for years untold, shared with generosity, their culture manifold. Yet the Europeans' expectations, rooted in foreign land, misunderstood this giving, and the seeds were sown in sand.

The Europeans saw sovereignty in laws of parchment ink, While the Wampanoag followed nature's lead, a sacred link. Their understanding of the earth, their bond with sky and sea, clashed with the newcomers' expectations, a cultural disharmony.

In dress and language, in customs and belief, The Wampanoag and Europeans, their differences were brief. But the misunderstandings, like ripples in a pond, drove wedges between them, as the world went on.

In two worlds colliding, with hopes and fears aglow, misunderstandings, like river currents, both fast and slow. Yet in their meetings, their hopes remained alive, to bridge the gaps of culture, and in harmony, to strive. The miscommunications, like clouds, would pass with time, as both cultures sought to learn, to bridge the gap, to climb.

The void left by Silvia and Tautog's disappearance created destruction. Tautog was held in almost a godlike way. He had brought many new advances to the people and had helped orchestrate fair trade with the Europeans. Now that he was gone, the ancient fire and vigor had died out with him. The men were tired and they were in bad shape. With no young leader to take the reins, Metacom had to find new warriors. John, a once vivid member of Plymouth, fell silently away to his musings and books after the disappearance of Silvia. John knew where they had gone, but that didn't stop the pains of sorrow he must endure.

John's prophecy about the colony suffering after Silvia left took on a deeper and more ominous meaning as events unfolded. Silvia's departure contributed to a sense of loss and instability in the colony. Without her calming presence and the unique bond, she shared with Tautog, the colonists found themselves more vulnerable to the tensions and conflicts that led to the outbreak of the war.

King Philip's War was a complex and devastating conflict between Native American tribes in New England and English settlers. Tensions had been simmering for years due to disputes over land ownership and encroachment on Native American territories. As European settlers expanded their presence in New England, Native Americans were often pushed off their ancestral lands.

Cultural clashes and religious differences between the English Puritans and Native American tribes added to the discord. The English sought to convert Native Americans to Christianity, which further strained relations. Metacom, also known as King Philip, was a Wampanoag leader who became a key figure in the conflict. He sought to unite various Native American tribes against English colonists and led the resistance against encroachment. A series of violent incidents and confrontations between Native Americans and English settlers escalated tensions. Acts of violence on both sides contributed to a cycle of retaliation.

In Plymouth, the execution of three Wampanoag men accused of murdering an Englishman in 1675 further inflamed hostilities. Metacom and his followers viewed this as an act of aggression. Metacom worked to form a coalition of Native American tribes, including the Nipmuck, Narragansett, and others, to resist English expansion. This alliance sought to coordinate efforts against the colonists.

In June 1675, hostilities erupted into open warfare. The conflict was marked by brutal battles, the destruction of English settlements, and the displacement of populations. It became one of the deadliest and most destructive conflicts in colonial American history.

King Philip's War resulted in significant loss of life and property on both sides, and it left a lasting impact on New England. The war marked the decline of Native American power and authority in the region and had far-reaching consequences for the relationship between Native Americans and English colonists.

The war, marked by brutal battles, the destruction of villages, and significant casualties on both sides, undoubtedly added to the suffering of the colony. The Native men sought to prove themselves for the position in the tribe that Tautog left behind. The tribal leadership was aging and growing insecure. Sixty years of pent-up aggression flowed during this time. Finally, peace came.

The Thanksgiving in 1676 was a somber and reflective occasion for the colonists. The war, which had resulted in significant loss of life and widespread destruction, had left a lasting impact on the New England colonies. In the aftermath of such a devastating conflict, the colonists gathered for a Thanksgiving observance with a sense of gratitude for their survival and resilience, despite the hardships they had endured.

The Thanksgiving feast in the wake of King Philip's War included the staples of the time, such as roasted meats, corn dishes, pumpkins, and other locally grown foods. However, the mood of the gathering was more subdued, with a focus on communal healing and rebuilding.

The war's toll on both the Native American tribes and the English settlers would have been in the minds of those in attendance, and the observance of Thanksgiving served as a moment of reflection on the challenges and conflicts that had tested their communities.

As modern-day Plymouth was rocked by the surprising news of Philip's engagement, the reverberations of this significant event sent shockwaves through history. In the past, these tremors were felt more subtly, like a small earthquake, causing ripples in time.

In the colonial era, John sat on his front porch, rocking gently in his chair, enjoying the tranquility of his surroundings. The peaceful, rustic scenery of his time provided a stark contrast to the bustling, technologically advanced world that Silvia was experiencing with Philip.

As he rocked back and forth, John felt a slight rumbling beneath his feet, like the distant echoes of a storm. He paused for a moment, looking around with curiosity. The old trees swayed gently in the breeze, and the chirping of birds continued uninterrupted. John considered the tremor to be nothing more than the quirks of nature—perhaps a distant thunderclap or the earth settling.

Little did he know that the engagement of Philip and Silvia was altering the course of history, sending echoes of change through time and space, including his own quiet existence in the past.

The next morning, Philip and Silvia made their way downstairs to the dining area, where the tantalizing aroma of freshly cooked pancakes greeted them. Philip's mother had prepared a delicious breakfast for the two of them, and it was a warm, inviting sight.

As they entered the room, Philip's father sat at the table, engrossed in his tablet, catching up on the latest news and updates from the outside world. He looked up from the screen, offering a brief nod of acknowledgment as he recognized his son's presence.

What truly caught Philip's parents off guard was the newfound wisdom and transformation they saw in their son. Philip had undergone a profound change since his journey with Silvia, and his demeanor exuded a newfound confidence and insight. It was as if he had experienced a lifetime of learning without letting on.

As they gathered around the table, Philip paused and, to the shock of his parents, offered a Christian prayer of grace over the meal. His mother, in particular, was taken aback and nearly lost her balance, so unexpected was this display of faith and reverence. Silvia, still overwhelmed from her incredible journey through time, watched this scene with a mixture of awe and surprise.

The breakfast table had become a place where not only pancakes were served but also a moment where the threads of time, faith, and wisdom were woven together, binding past and present in ways that defied ordinary understanding. In 2050, most emotions were felt by humans and were a profound experience, however, their minds were always in control thanks to the successful development of brain chip-implants. The implants explained why Silvia felt like such an outsider. The rest of the family had updated and timely information sent to their chips so they would stay in "the know." The chip implants also explained Weetamoo's discord and feeling off-balance at a spiritual encounter.

The monthly chip implant ritual had become an integral part of Philip's family's life in the year 2050. These remarkable technological enhancements were designed to keep individuals updated with the latest advancements in science, math, and technology. The chips communicated directly with their brains, providing knowledge and insights that altered their perspective on life without diminishing their unique personalities.

Silvia was astounded when the Tautog family told her what their secret was. She had never heard of such a device, and could hardly begin to understand the technology that went into having one. Philip told her not to worry, that she would have one as well soon enough.

One crisp morning, the family gathered in their spacious, high-tech living room. The delivery drone, adorned with a sleek metallic design, descended gracefully onto the balcony, carrying the monthly package of chip implants. Philip's parents, with an air of anticipation, opened the package, revealing the small, unobtrusive devices that would be implanted shortly.

Philip explained the process to Silvia, emphasizing the benefits of this technology and how it had helped them adapt and thrive in the future world. He assured her that it wouldn't change who she was but would provide her with valuable knowledge to navigate their new reality.

With a sense of curiosity and trepidation, Silvia agreed to the implantation, recognizing that her journey through time had brought her to a world where such innovations were essential. As Philip's family prepared to undergo the procedure, they understood that their minds would soon be enriched with the latest insights and knowledge, ensuring they could adapt to the ever-evolving world of the 21st century.

The day arrived for Silvia to receive the chip implant, a pivotal moment in her journey into the future. She had witnessed the incredible advances of this era, from flying hoverboards to electric vehicles like Philip's Tesla. However, she still lacked a comprehensive understanding of the underlying technology that powered these marvels.

Silvia lay on a comfortable examination table, the sterile, high-tech room around her filled with futuristic medical equipment. A skilled technician prepared her for the procedure, ensuring her comfort and well-being.

As the chip was implanted, Silvia felt a brief, but not uncomfortable, sensation. The process was remarkably quick and painless. The chip interfaced with her brain, connecting her to a wealth of knowledge and information. Her world began to shift in subtle yet profound ways.

With the new implant, Silvia's understanding of the world expanded exponentially. She now had insights into the intricate workings of flying hoverboards and electric vehicles. The chip allowed her to grasp the principles of electromagnetism, propulsion, and aerodynamics, shedding light on how these incredible technologies functioned.

In addition to understanding the mechanics of the modern world, Silvia's chip provided her with a deep dive into genetics. She could unravel the intricacies of DNA, genetic engineering, and heredity with astonishing clarity. This knowledge transformed her perspective on life, evolution, and the potential for advancements in medical science.

As Silvia absorbed this newfound understanding, she felt a profound sense of awe and wonder for the possibilities of the future. Her chip implant had opened doors to knowledge she had never imagined, allowing her to bridge the gap between her historical roots and the boundless potential of the 21st century.

As the days grew warmer, Silvia's curiosity and passion for understanding the marvels of the 21st century continued to blossom. Inspired by the pioneering work of Gregor Mendel in the field of genetics, she decided to experiment with gene editing in the garden. Armed with her newfound knowledge and the capabilities provided by her chip implant, she embarked on a fascinating journey of genetic exploration.

Silvia selected a young tree in the garden and carefully began her experiment. With precision and care, she harnessed the power of genetic engineering to introduce modifications to the tree's DNA. Her goal was ambitious—to grow multiple types of fruit on the same tree within days.

As she applied her newfound genetic insights, the tree responded to her interventions with remarkable speed. Within a matter of days, it bore fruit that was only just an idea in her mind. This gave her confidence into her new skills and ingenuity. Branches adorned with a medley of different fruits—apples, pears, peaches, and more—grew side by side on the same tree. The vibrant colors and delicious aromas filled the garden with a sense of wonder and amazement.

Silvia's achievement was a testament to her determination, her adaptability, and the boundless possibilities that the future held. She had bridged the gap between her historical knowledge and the cutting-edge technologies of the 21st century, creating a garden that was not only bountiful but a living force privy to the power of human ingenuity and the wonders of genetic engineering.

Philip observed Silvia's daily pursuits in the garden with great pride and admiration. Her successes in various projects were a source of joy and wonder for him, as they showcased her determination and adaptability in embracing the technological advances. His parents were just as thrilled with her progress as they were inspired. Philip and Silvia's love was optimistic, happy, and full of energy. They secretly vowed to begin their own interesting projects.

Philip marveled at her ability to harness the power of genetic engineering and create a garden that bore multiple types of fruit on a single tree. He did not know what was the driving force behind this experiment, but he was certainly glad it didn't end in a two-headed goat.

Meanwhile, Philip was channeling his own efforts into the world of digital finance. In a world defined by technological advancements, he immersed himself in the complexities of digital currencies, blockchain technology, and financial innovations. His work in the field was marked by a dedication to understanding and navigating the financial landscape of the time.

As a couple, Philip and Silvia represented a beautiful fusion of the past and the future, each contributing their unique strengths and expertise to create a harmonious partnership that spanned the ages. Their shared journey through time had brought them to a world of endless possibilities, and they continued to thrive in this dynamic and ever-evolving future.

Spring slowly unfurled its vibrant colors, as the world awakened from its Wintry slumber. The days grew longer, and nature's symphony filled the air with the sweet melodies of birdsong and the fragrant scents of blossoms. In this season of renewal, Silvia and Philip prepared for a momentous occasion that would bind their lives together in a lavish wedding.

Their wedding day arrived in a swirl of excitement and joy, as friends and family gathered to celebrate the union of two souls from different eras. The venue was adorned with spring flowers in full bloom, and the air was filled with a sense of anticipation and love.

Philip stood at the altar, his eyes fixed on Silvia, radiant in her elegant white gown. Her veil was floor length and had rosettes adorning the edges. The soft glow of the candles in the church flickered, casting a warm ambiance. Silvia's eyes sparkled with joy and anticipation as she held a bouquet of flowers, a mix of modern and traditional blooms.

Philip, dressed in a tailored suit that echoed the classic style of his historical roots but with a modern twist, his hair slicked back and shining like black stone. He took Silvia's hand in his. The church seemed to hold its breath in anticipation of the vows that would bind them together.

Philip's voice resonated through the hallowed space as he spoke words filled with love and commitment. His vows were a blend of promises inspired by the enduring values of the past and a vision of a shared future. The sincerity in his eyes and the tenderness of his words echoed the timeless sentiments that transcended the centuries.

Silvia, with tears of joy glistening in her eyes, listened intently as Philip expressed his deepest emotions. The air in the church was filled with a sense of unity, as if the echoes of centuries past whispered their blessings on this union that bridged the gap between history and the present.

As they exchanged rings, the atmosphere became charged with the shared emotions of the couple and the collective spirit of those who had witnessed countless vows in that sacred space. The timeless beauty of the ceremony encapsulated the essence of their love, transcending the boundaries of time and culture. Their marriage was sanctified in the Church and almost cataloged amongst the saintly paintings that adorned the walls.

The newlyweds looked at each other and realized they did not need anyone else in the room. They were a united front, a forever circle of love, and an item to be certain.

A lavish feast followed the ceremony, and the celebration continued late into the evening. Yet, amidst the laughter and dancing, there was a bittersweet note that echoed in their hearts. John's absence was deeply felt, and both Silvia and Philip longed for his presence on this momentous day.

In the quiet moments, as they gazed at the starry sky, Philip's thoughts turned to his father and his ancestral lineage. He felt a powerful connection to his roots, yet a pang of sadness that he couldn't share the news of his journey and the life he had built with Silvia with anyone. This realization brought them closer, knowing that their love had transcended time and that they were building a life together that bridged the past and the future.

Silvia and Philip's love story had a depth and richness that went beyond the boundaries of time, and it was a source of inspiration and wonder for all who were fortunate enough to witness it. In the Spring's embrace, they tied the knot, two souls entwined, a love that never forgot. Amidst the blooms, and nature's sweet song, they pledged their love, so pure and strong.

In a lavish affair, their hearts took flight, beneath the stars, their love burned bright. but in their joy, there lingered a trace, of absent friends, and a father's embrace. As Silvia and Philip danced the night away at a lavish gala, surrounded by elegance and celebration, Silvia couldn't help but be swept away by the grandeur of the moment. The exquisite setting, the dazzling lights, and the music that filled the air all contributed to a sense of enchantment.

In the midst of the splendor, Silvia's thoughts drifted back in time to her mother, Sarah, and her wedding day. She wondered if this was how her mother had felt on that special occasion. The dance floor, the laughter, and the shared joy with loved ones might have mirrored the sentiments that Sarah had experienced during her wedding.

Silvia's connection with the past had deepened since her journey through time, and she felt a profound sense of unity with her ancestors, imagining the joy and love that had filled her family's history. This moment of reflection added a layer of nostalgia to the gala, making it a poignant and unforgettable evening.

During their honeymoon, Silvia and John embarked on a journey through history, teaching Silvia about the events and developments that had unfolded in the last 400 years. They began with the American Revolutionary War, a pivotal moment in the nation's history. Silvia absorbed the knowledge with a sense of wonder, realizing the immense changes that had occurred since she had left her time.

As they delved into the pages of history, Silvia couldn't help but consider her father's fate. She understood that, in her time, he may not have survived to witness King Philip's War and the challenges it brought. Yet, she was content to imagine that the rest of his life played out in comfort and happiness within their cabin, far away from the tumultuous events of that period.

The couple's honeymoon was not only a celebration of their love but also an exploration of the vast expanse of time and the shared history that bound them. It was a journey through the ages, filled with tales of courage, change, and the enduring spirit of humanity, as they embarked on a new chapter in their lives together.

As Silvia delved deeper into the annals of history during her honeymoon with John, she discovered a heartwarming and significant development in the more recent past. She learned that, in 1924, her people had championed the cause of Native Americans, advocating for their recognition as full citizens and acknowledging their integral role in the history of the original colony.

Silvia was filled with a sense of marvel and pride as she grasped the magnitude of this accomplishment. Her small and humble colony had grown to become a symbol of unity and inclusiveness, acknowledging the contributions and rights of the Native American population. Her little village was the blueprint to the values and principles that had evolved over the centuries, fostering a spirit of cooperation, understanding, and equity which now formed the United States of America.

The history she learned was a digital token of the enduring capacity of people to evolve, change, and strive for a more inclusive and compassionate world. It added another layer of appreciation to her understanding of her people and the legacy they had created in the span of four centuries.

In the months that followed, Silvia continued to immerse herself in the history and culture of the 21st century, making it her own. She adapted to her new life in 2051, embracing the opportunities and challenges it brought. With John by her side, she officially became a citizen of this time, marking her place in a world that had evolved over four centuries.

As life moved forward, a beautiful and life-altering development occurred—Silvia discovered that she was with child. It was a moment of immense joy and significance, and it brought a deep sense of fulfillment and continuity. Silvia couldn't help but think back to her royal lineage and the legacy she carried with her into the future.

Silvia's days were filled with a special kind of anticipation as the news of her pregnancy spread joy throughout their home. The rustic cabin, now a blend of historical charm and modern comforts, became a hub of excitement and preparation.

Silvia, with a gentle glow about her, moved gracefully through the rooms adorned with both traditional and contemporary elements. The fireplace crackled with warmth, casting a cozy ambiance over the space. Philip, beaming with pride, helped Silvia arrange a nursery that merged the simplicity of the past with the conveniences of the present.

In one corner, a cradle crafted with care echoed the craftsmanship of bygone eras, while nearby, a modern crib stood ready with its sleek design. Silvia, with a touch of nostalgia, hung handmade quilts on the walls—a nod to the past, a gift from the Wampanoag tribe. The room spoke of a harmonious blend, a testament to the love that spanned centuries.

Silvia's days were a delightful dance between reading age-old parenting books and exploring new digital resources on child-rearing. The shelves were filled with a collection of both, creating a bridge between the wisdom of generations. As she prepared meals in the kitchen, the aroma of traditional Native American dishes mingled with the contemporary scents of her modern cooking.

The changing seasons outside mirrored the changes within Silvia. In the evenings, she and Philip would sit by the fireplace, discussing the future and reminiscing about their unique journey through time. The cabin echoed with laughter, stories, and the hum of preparations for the newest member of their family.

As the due date approached, the cabin seemed to hold its breath in anticipation, ready to welcome a new life that would embody the beautiful union of the past and the present.

Chapter Seven- A Baby's Ability

ON THANKSGIVING DAY in 2051, Silvia and Philip welcomed their precious baby boy into the world, and their hearts swelled with gratitude and joy. The day held even deeper significance now, as it marked the arrival of the newest addition to their family.

Their son's nursery was a testament to the holiday that had brought them together in the past and the love that would shape his future. It was adorned with Thanksgiving-themed decor, with vibrant autumn leaves, cornucopias, and a warm color palette that filled the room with a sense of coziness and celebration.

As Silvia held their newborn son in her arms, she couldn't help but think of the incredible journey that had brought her to this moment. The past and the future converged in this nursery, where traditions of old were passed down to a new generation.

Their baby boy, a symbol of love. He was a gift, not only to Silvia and Philip but to the world, a symbol of hope and the endless possibilities that lay ahead in this ever-evolving future. The annual Tautog Thanksgiving celebration in 2051 was a grand and joyous affair. It brought together friends and family from near and far, all gathering to commemorate the holiday and the cherished traditions it represented. This year, the celebration held an even more special significance, as Silvia and Philip's baby was due to make his entrance into the world.

As the celebration continued, Silvia went into labor, and the guests could sense the anticipation and excitement in the air. With the support of her loving husband, Philip, and the guidance of modern medicine, Silvia gave birth to their baby boy right there at the heart of the Thanksgiving celebration.

The guests, surrounded by the warmth of the holiday and the sense of unity that Thanksgiving embodied, broke into cheers and applause when they heard the news of the newborn's arrival. Their joy was palpable as they offered their heartfelt congratulations to the new parents.

Tautog, who had become a dear friend and a bridge between the past and the present, beamed with pride as he witnessed the birth of this new generation. The Tautog Thanksgiving had always been a time for reflection, gratitude, and unity, and now it had become a symbol of the enduring spirit of family and the power of love.

The annual celebration took on a new layer of significance, marking the birth of a child who represented the fusion of past and present, and the promise of a bright and united future. It was a day that would be cherished for generations to come, a testament to the enduring power of Thanksgiving and the connections that bind us across time and space.

Silvia and Philip faced the challenges of parenting with a deep sense of unity and shared history. Their journey had been a remarkable one, spanning centuries, and it had brought them together in a way that was unlike any other. As they navigated the complexities of parenthood, they found solace and strength in the experiences they had shared.

Their shared past experiences were a constant source of connection and understanding. Silvia's upbringing in the 17th century and Philip's life in the 21st century created a unique blend of perspectives, traditions, and values that enriched their parenting journey. They found themselves learning from each other every day, blending the wisdom of generations with the innovation of the present.

They fell in love all over again each day as they saw the beauty of their son growing and evolving. Silvia marveled at the modern world and the opportunities it offered their child. Their love was a fusion of the past and the present, a celebration of the enduring connection that bound them together.

Through the challenges and joys of parenthood. Their love story continued to evolve, marked by a deep sense of gratitude and wonder, as they embraced the past, lived in the present, and looked forward to a future filled with hope and promise.

Silvia and Philip chose the name "Wolf" for their precious baby boy. It was a name that held a sense of strength, courage, and a connection to the natural world, embracing both the past and the present.

As Wolf grew and reached the age for his chip implant, the process was designed to be gentle, gradually bringing information into his awareness as he matured. However, like many children, the experience could be overwhelming. When Wolf received his chip implant, he cried, his tiny face scrunched up in confusion and discomfort. The implant was meant to open up a world of knowledge, but to the young child, it felt like an intrusion into his peaceful existence.

Silvia and Philip comforted their son, soothing his tears and reassuring him that this new knowledge would become a source of wonder and discovery. The young boy's cries were a reminder of the challenges and adjustments that came with each generation, but they also represented the hope and potential of the future.

As they held Wolf in their arms, they knew that he would grow to embrace the knowledge and opportunities that this modern world offered, just as they had learned to appreciate the wisdom of the past.

The mystery surrounding Wolf's reaction to his chip implant deepened as he continued to cry even a year after the implantation. Concerned, the doctors decided to hook him up to a monitor to better understand what might be causing his distress. What they discovered left them baffled and intrigued.

The monitor revealed that Wolf's unique chip implant allowed him to perceive both the past and the present simultaneously. He seemed to have an extraordinary ability to access not only the knowledge brought by the implant but also the collective memories of the past, seamlessly interwoven with the modern world around him.

This phenomenon was a psychological enigma that had never been observed before. It left doctors and experts in awe and wonder at the complexity of the human mind and the potential of technology to unlock new dimensions of perception.

As Silvia and Philip watched their son navigate this extraordinary ability, they knew that Wolf was destined for a remarkable journey, one that would bridge the past and the present in a way that defied understanding. It was a testament to the enduring power of human consciousness and the uncharted territories that the future held, waiting to be explored by the generations to come.

The doctors were astounded by the capabilities of Wolf's chip implant, which seemed to function like a split screen, allowing him to process information from both the past and the present simultaneously. It was as if he was bridging gaps in time and perception, offering a unique glimpse into the complex workings of human consciousness.

Recognizing the potential significance of Wolf's abilities, the doctors reached out to a tech investor who was intrigued by the possibilities. The investor decided to support the family by providing them with specialized monitors that allowed them to witness, in real time, the past, present, and future through Wolf's life and understanding.

This innovative technology was a breakthrough that opened up new horizons for the family and for humanity as a whole. As they explored the past, saw the present, and glimpsed into the future through Wolf's extraordinary perspective, they began to realize the profound potential for greater understanding and insight.

The journey that lay ahead was filled with questions and discoveries, offering a glimpse into the limitless possibilities that the fusion of human consciousness and advanced technology could unlock. Wolf's unique abilities were a testament to the ever-evolving nature of human potential, and the future held endless mysteries waiting to be unraveled.

The astral projections enabled by the specialized monitors took an astonishing turn when one day, as Silvia and her family explored the past, they encountered a familiar figure. There, in one of the monitors equipped with sound, appeared John Alden, seated in his rocking chair. Silvia's heart skipped a beat as she saw her father, a cherished figure from her past, brought back to life in this extraordinary way.

However, John Alden remained unaware of their presence. He could not see or hear Silvia and her family as they observed him from the future. The technology allowed them to witness his moments, his expressions, and the everyday life he had lived, creating a profound connection between past and present.

For Silvia, this was a bittersweet revelation. She had longed to see her father again, and now she had the opportunity to observe his life in a way she could never have imagined. The astral projections opened up a window to the past, allowing her to glimpse the man who had shaped her life and her understanding of the world.

As they continued to watch, the connection between past and present grew stronger, and Silvia felt a sense of both comfort and longing. The past and the future were intertwined in a way that was beyond the scope of imagination, and the possibilities for exploration and understanding were endless.

The extraordinary ability of Wolf's chip implant to bridge time and perception was like a manifestation of the love and shared memories that Silvia and Philip had forged throughout their unique journey. It seemed to be engrained in Wolf's very DNA, a testament to the enduring power of their connection and the seamless way it brought time together.

Recognizing the immense potential of this newfound ability, a team of technology experts and scientists came over to the family's home, eager to further explore and improve upon this remarkable phenomenon. Their goal was to enhance and refine the technology, ensuring that Wolf's chip implant could provide even more valuable insights into the past, present, and future.

With the help of these dedicated tech experts, Silvia, Philip, and their son, Wolf, embarked on a journey of discovery that would not only deepen their understanding of the human mind but also unlock a wealth of knowledge and insight about the interconnectedness of time and consciousness.

As they delved deeper into the possibilities of this extraordinary technology, they were poised to unveil a new chapter in the story of human evolution, one that transcended the boundaries of time and allowed them to experience the past, embrace the present, and explore the future with unprecedented clarity and understanding.

At night, Philip and Silvia dissected what was happening to their son. He was able to unlock different moments in time and space. There, it was quiet and slow-motion understanding was a feature of the new technology he was building. This meant that in essence, humans could learn from even micro-moments and find peace in every situation's situation.

Her son's experience and seemingly spontaneous growth intrigued Silvia. She could not help but draw the analogy to the baby Jesus saving humanity. If anyone thought this type of technology and scientific advancement was possible, it would not have been Silvia.

John Alden often found solace in visiting the tree where they had discovered his daughter's shoes, a place that had become a silent memorial in its own right. It was a remarkable symbol of her extraordinary journey through time, and the fact that she had not perished was a source of constant encouragement and joy for him.

The tree had taken on the role of a headstone, marking the spot where Silvia had vanished into the mysteries of time. However, instead of being a place of mourning, it had become a testament to her resilience and the enduring spirit of their family. John visited this tree daily, where he found a deep connection to the divine, offering his gratitude and prayers.

The tree not only provided John with a sense of connection to his daughter but also gave him a renewed sense of life and purpose. It was a symbol of the unbreakable bond between them, and a reminder that, even when separated by centuries, their love and connection continued to thrive.

As John prayed beneath the tree, he felt a profound sense of gratitude and hope, knowing that Silvia's story was far from over, and that their paths, though divergent in time, remained intertwined in ways that were both mysterious and beautiful.

As John's life continued to unfold, he found unexpected love and companionship in the most unlikely of places. During a Thanksgiving meal, he met a Native woman who captured his heart and, in turn, had her heart captured by him. Their connection deepened, and she eventually moved into his cabin, bridging the gap between their two worlds.

Over time, the Native woman embraced Christianity and adopted European fashion, a transformation that John found both endearing and novel. Their love and companionship brought newfound joy and meaning into John's life, and he cherished the opportunity to care for and be cared for by this remarkable woman.

John and his wife, deeply moved by the inexplicable miracles unfolding beneath the extraordinary tree, began to hold prayer services in its presence. The townspeople initially regarded John's actions with a mixture of curiosity and skepticism, believing that he might have lost his mind to what they perceived as mere superstition.

However, one fateful day, during a prayer service beneath the miraculous tree, an astounding event occurred that left the entire community in awe. A baby's cry resonated through the air, filling the hearts of all who were present with a sense of wonder and reverence. The townspeople, once skeptical, now found themselves united in their belief that something extraordinary was happening in their midst.

The baby's cry was a symbol of hope and the miraculous power of faith, and it served to strengthen the bond of the community, bringing them together in shared wonder and gratitude for the unexplainable wonders of life and time that unfolded beneath the branches of the remarkable tree.

The tree that had become a silent memorial to Silvia's extraordinary journey continued to astound and inspire John with its remarkable transformations. One day, as he approached the tree, he was greeted by the sight of enormous lemons dangling from its branches. The following day, big, juicy apples appeared, each one a juicy product of the tree's mysterious nature.

For an entire month, the tree continued to yield different types of fruits, each more unusual and exotic than the last. The ever-changing bounty of the tree piqued John's curiosity and filled him with a sense of wonder. It was as if the tree itself were a living testament to the passage of time, offering new surprises and revelations each day.

John couldn't help but take notice of the tree's unique gifts, which seemed to be a living connection to the past, the present, and the future. It was a reminder that even in the most unexpected places, the mysteries of life and time could bring forth beauty and wonder, continuously renewing existence.

As John waited patiently near the tree, the world around him seemed to blur in the anticipation of the miraculous. And then, as if a dream come true, he heard the sweet, melodic voice of his beloved daughter, Silvia. "Dad, can you hear us?" Her voice rang out, carrying with it an overwhelming sense of joy and relief.

John's heart soared as he responded, his voice trembling with emotion, "Silvia, my baby. Can you hear me?" The reply came swiftly and lovingly, "Yes, Dad." It was a moment of profound reunion, a result of the enduring power of love and the inexplicable wonders that connected their lives across the boundaries of time and existence.

Tears of joy streamed down John's face as he realized that, in the most extraordinary way, he was once again in communion with his beloved daughter, Silvia, whose journey through time had brought them back together in a bond that defied the limitations of the past, present, and future.

In a world where time's embrace unfolds, a toddler named Wolf, a tale to be told. With innocence pure, in wonder he stood, a child of the present, linked to the past's hood. Tiny fingers, curious eyes wide, a chip implanted, secrets to confide. Whispers of epochs in his tiny ear, the dance of history, crystal clear.

In the nursery adorned with care, Wolf, a traveler through time's rare air. Chubby cheeks and laughter sweet, a connection profound, both past and fleet. Through the chip's magic, a bridge he'd weave, between moments in time, a dream to believe. In the quiet of night, in the soft nursery glow, Wolf interacted with a world's ebb and flow.

A giggle echoed through the ancient years, as the chip unveiled laughter, joy, and tears. Past and present entwined in his gaze, a toddler exploring the time-traveling maze. Footsteps of ancestors, whispers of lore, Wolf danced with history, forevermore. With each babble and each playful cry, he touched the threads where memories lie.

Every wobbled step he took, a first of this new frontier. Every knee did bow, ever animal to hear. The universe herself shifted slightly to meet his gait, knowing now that there was never really an idea called fate.

In the soft moonlight, a lullaby sung, a tale of a toddler, whose heart was young. Past and present, a celestial ballet, Wolf, the time-traveling toddler, led the way.

Chapter Eight- Pease Talks and Treaties

THE TOWNSPEOPLE AND the tribe could not believe what they were hearing. This magic tree had also produced the sounds of John's family. He was in awe and did not know where to attribute the glory except to God.

John's wife knelt beside the tree. She humbly prayed, and as she did so, John could hear his daughter's voice telling him she was in the year 2050. Astounded, John held onto his wife so he would not fall over.

"Silvia, my dear, are you alright?" His voice was shaking with emotion.

"Yes! You would not believe the future! Our people have worked together all this time to create an almost Heaven-like existence!" Silvia exclaimed. Her voice was coming through soft and frail, as if it would disappear altogether at any moment.

"Heaven-like?" John asked.

"Yes, papa. It is a world where there are many people, disease is rare, and there are so many interesting and unique inventions." Silvia went on.

John paused briefly to image what she was saying. "Tell us more!"

"I cannot tonight, papa. Wolf is getting tired and the connection is fading. Meet us here tomorrow at the same time?" Silvia asked.

"We will do it!" Her dad replied. Soon, the transmission was over. The townspeople all gathered together and looked reverently at John. They all agreed this was not witchcraft, yet, unbelievable. They sat in silence absorbing the message for a few minutes before getting up and stretching. A silent promise filled the room that they would meet here again tomorrow at the same time.

John and his wife made their way back to the cabin. John, being the therapist that he was, was in tune with the thoughts and feelings of his neighbors. They were all astounded by what just happened. Many were excited, and some were fearful. John knew that listening to Silvia would led the tribe in a common direction of work and harmony.

While John's time met with hope and faith in the future, Silvia's time met on the other side for gratitude and remembrance.

In the hush of twilight, Silvia cradled Wolf in her arms, a tiny vessel of wonder, untouched by life's violent harms. His eyes, a canvas of innocence and glee, reflecting the magic of the past, the present's jubilee.

The room bathed in a gentle, warm glow, as Silvia hummed a melody, soft and slow. A quilt woven with tales from eras bygone, wrapped around Wolf, a legacy to dawn. With a delicate touch, she laid him down to rest, tucked in his crib, by love deeply blessed. his tiny breaths, a cadence of dreams, as the moon whispered secrets in soft moonbeam streams.

Silvia gazed at Wolf, a peaceful cherub in sleep, a tiny traveler whose journey was deep. The room echoed with the lull of night, as past and present converged in soft, celestial light. A mother's love, a timeless embrace, as Wolf slumbered in the tapestry of time's grace. Silvia lingered, a guardian in the quiet, watching over her child, a celestial delight.

In the stillness, the room held a tale, of a toddler's dreams, where past and present set sail. Silvia, a weaver of moments, a keeper of lore, guarding Wolf's dreams as the night's essence bore. Silvia was a kind and devoted mother. Each night she prayed for the ability and patience to wait for Wolf to tell her his private dreams. She believed that these dreams would unlock endless possibilities and directions for a peaceful and prosperous future for mankind.

In the quiet dawn of Plymouth's morn, John, with determination, faced a task unborn. A projector screen, a portal to traverse, to glimpse his daughter, a bond to immerse.

He sought metal, sturdy and true, canvases to capture the ethereal view. Crystals, the magic conduits to employ, to bridge the gap, connect past and present's joy. A craftsman's vision, a father's plea, to transcend the confines of time's decree. In the heart of the colony, a workshop arose, a haven of dreams where hope securely grows.

With calloused hands and a determined stare, John fashioned a screen with meticulous care. Metal frames intertwined like a dance, a bridge to Silvia's world, a fateful chance. Canvases stretched, a blank tableau, awaiting the stories time would bestow. Crystals aligned, a celestial array, to capture images from the sun's new day.

As the sun ascended in the azure sky, John's creation took shape, reaching high. A portal to link two worlds unseen, a father's endeavor, a projector screen. In the hush of the afternoon's embrace, John tested the device, hope on his face. Crystals shimmered, canvases alive, a connection sought, love to revive.

With bated breath and a heart sincere, He gazed upon the screen, a pioneer. Silvia's world beckoned, a spectral gleam, through the woven magic of the projector screen.

Finally, John had his makeshift projector screens ready. He and some townspeople carried them to the edge of the forest on horseback. They spent the morning setting them near the tree and aligning the with the afternoon sun. They were able to take small wires and create a charge (the begins of modern electricity), and plug them into the tree. Silvia's voice came through the tree loud and strong.

The townspeople waited for exhausting minutes to see if their contraption would hold true. The electrical current from the tree was siphoned into the projectors through the primitive wires, and the screens began to flash. It was a miracle! The light from the sun was converting into electrical signals! It was helping the tree prosper, and the canvas was acting as a screen to show the change!

This was an interesting find; however, it was not able to produce images from the future. John and the rest of the people settled down in their seats as they listened to Silvia's melodic voice.

She spoke of wars, inventions, and countries that no one could believe. She told them about the brain chips and the tree she created. People were left in amazement that the tree in their forest was becoming the tree in Silvia's world. This fact seemed to prove that time shifting on a global scale was also possible.

Finally, she told them about Wolf and his special ability to make this communication possible. She was matter-of-fact and uplifting in her message. After all of this had time to resonate with the people, John held a meeting to discuss this progress.

"Clearly, Silvia is telling the truth," John began. "She wants to see this colony prosper, and it is a fact that we do. I don't know how we are going to achieve what Silvia said is possible, but we must." The people agreed and all went home with a new idea of what the future could hold. Each person felt the weight of their own responsibility and worth.

Philip went to bed that night proud of his wife for motivating the people with her message of truth. She was rallying her family up for a future so amazing, none of them could believe it. This was in fact one small step for man, and a giant lead for mankind.

Philip lay in bed that night thinking about the intricacies and frailties of life. He realized his work was magnanimous, and he needed to tell others and get help. What if there was a place so vast and large that the peoples of the past, present, and future could live on the same plane in unity? Philip and Silvia sat at the breakfast table, a warm and inviting scene in their modern home. The morning sun streamed through the windows, casting a gentle glow on the family gathered around. Little Wolf, their toddler, sat in a high chair, eagerly awaiting his morning meal.

Silvia, inspired by the idea of democracy that had evolved over centuries, looked at Philip with a thoughtful expression. The realization had dawned on her, a spark of insight fueled by the morning light and the love surrounding their family. She believed that in a true democracy, every voice should be heard, and the process of voting should be simple and accessible.

As they fed Wolf, passing bites of breakfast back and forth, Silvia shared her newfound perspective with Philip. Her eyes sparkled with enthusiasm as she spoke about the importance of inclusivity and the ease with which people should be able to express their opinions in a democracy.

Philip, always attentive to Silvia's ideas, listened with a smile. He admired her passion and nodded in agreement, appreciating the depth of thought that Silvia brought to their conversations. The family scene was a blend of ordinary moments and profound reflections, a testament to the evolving nature of their lives and the enduring values they held dear.

In the midst of this simple and pleasant interchange, Silvia's vision for democracy took root—a seed planted in the rich soil of their shared experiences, nourished by the love and understanding that bound them together.

Silvia, driven by her vision of a more inclusive democracy, sat down at her computer, tapping into the modern marvels of technology that surrounded her in the year 2051. With the familiar hum of the device and the glow of the screen, she connected to the communal thoughts page of the Brain Chip website.

As she navigated through the digital interface, Silvia's fingers danced over the keyboard with purpose. Her coding skills, honed over time, allowed her to create a section where people could collectively think about the concept of voting for issues and leaders securely on the internet. This innovative idea stemmed from her belief in the power of technology to amplify the voices of the people.

Silvia envisioned a space where individuals could share their thoughts, concerns, and aspirations for a more accessible and participatory democratic process. The communal thoughts page became a virtual agora, a meeting place for ideas and discussions that transcended the boundaries of time and space.

Her coding work was meticulous, weaving together the threads of technological advancement and democratic ideals. Silvia's commitment to fostering a sense of community and shared governance shone through as she introduced a platform for people to engage in collective deliberation.

Once her coding was complete, Silvia took a moment to reflect on the potential impact of her creation. The digital realm had become a canvas for her vision of a democracy that embraced the diversity of voices and empowered individuals to actively shape the future.

With a sense of accomplishment, Silvia eagerly shared her idea with Philip and the wider online community. The communal thoughts page, now enriched with the possibility of digital voting discussions, stood as a testament to Silvia's ongoing journey of bridging the past and the present in pursuit of a more equitable and inclusive future.

Silvia's insatiable curiosity and her determination to bridge the gap between past and present led her to embark on a new and captivating project. If she could make fruit appear in the past, she wondered, what other wonders could she bring to the world she had left behind?

With dedication and ingenuity, Silvia set out to introduce bioluminescence to the trees of Plymouth, using her knowledge and the capabilities of the future. Month after month, she labored tirelessly, and soon, her efforts bore fruit in the form of a radiant transformation.

As the days gave way to nights, the once ordinary Plymouth forest was bathed in a mesmerizing glow of bioluminescent light. The trees, aglow with a natural radiance, created a breathtaking spectacle that filled the hearts of all who beheld it with wonder and awe. The forest had been transformed into a living, magical dreamscape that transcended time itself.

Silvia's insatiable curiosity and unyielding spirit led her to venture even further into the realm of possibilities. She pondered the idea of transporting people or objects from the past into the future, driven by the desire to expand the horizons of what was achievable in her unique position.

Silvia's tireless commitment to building a brighter and more connected world rippled beyond the confines of her immediate community. Her innovative ideas and determination to bring people together became a beacon of inspiration, capturing the hearts and minds of those around her. The transformative impact of her work resonated far and wide, igniting a global conversation about the endless possibilities that lay ahead.

As Silvia's vision gained momentum, her neighbors and friends became ambassadors of change, sharing the story of her achievements and the collective dreams they now dared to dream. The once-muted whispers of possibility evolved into a resounding chorus, echoing through communities, cities, and nations.

The entire world buzzed with anticipation as people from diverse backgrounds, cultures, and experiences united under the banner of Silvia's vision. Her unwavering belief in the potential of technology to foster unity and amplify voices found resonance in the hearts of millions.

Silvia's journey, rooted in the rich tapestry of history, transcended temporal boundaries, weaving a narrative of hope, innovation, and human connection. Her legacy became a living testament to the idea that one person's determination could spark a global movement toward positive change.

In the wake of Silvia's transformative influence, the world witnessed a collective awakening. People began to explore new horizons, challenge conventional norms, and embrace the spirit of collaboration. The air was charged with the energy of possibility, and the once-distant dreams of a more inclusive and interconnected world seemed within reach.

Silvia's name became synonymous with the boundless potential of human imagination and the enduring power of community. Her story echoed through history, reminding future generations that the actions of a single individual could ripple across time, shaping the destiny of the world.

The global buzz surrounding Silvia's vision marked the dawn of a new era—one where innovation, unity, and the shared pursuit of a brighter future became the guiding principles for humanity's journey forward.

With unwavering determination, she dedicated the remaining days of her life to this ambitious endeavor. She meticulously crafted intricate code for people's implants, laying the groundwork for a future where time and space could be defied. Silvia understood that she might not live to witness the fruition of her work, but she had an unwavering hope that her efforts would one day bear fruit.

Silvia's legacy was not only the remarkable achievements she had already unlocked but the tantalizing possibility of future breakthroughs, waiting for the right minds to unlock the secrets of time and space, love and forgiveness.

Thanksgiving in the year Wolf became an adult was a celebration unlike any other. The Plymouth colony, now a thriving and technologically advanced community, gathered to express gratitude and enjoy the bounties of their lives. The air was filled with the savory aroma of a feast that combined traditional recipes with futuristic culinary creations.

In the Alden household, Philip and Silvia hosted the gathering, their home adorned with futuristic decorations and holographic displays. The dining table was set with a fusion of classic and modern dishes, reflecting the rich history and technological advancements of their time.

Wolf, now a grown man, had become a respected figure in the community. His chip implant, which once caused him to cry as a child, now served as a unique connection to the past and future. People sought his wisdom and insights, considering him a modern-day prophet.

As the family and community sat down for the Thanksgiving meal, Wolf expressed his gratitude for the harmonious blend of their shared past and present. The room echoed with laughter, conversations, and the clinking of glasses as they toasted to the blessings of the year.

The feast was a testament to the unity between the Pilgrims and the Wampanoag, symbolizing the strength that comes from embracing diversity and technological progress. As the community gave thanks, they reflected on their journey through time, cherishing the memories of the past and embracing the limitless possibilities of the future.

The Thanksgiving table stood as a symbol of abundance and prosperity in the Plymouth colony. As the community gathered around, a sense of unity and shared purpose filled the air. The holographic displays projected images of historical feasts and modern innovations, blending the past and present seamlessly.

The table, adorned with a fusion of traditional and futuristic dishes, reflected the diversity and richness of their lives. People from various backgrounds and walks of life sat side by side, eager to share their stories, knowledge, and dreams for the future.

As they indulged in the feast, the communal thoughts page of the Brain Chip website buzzed with discussions about innovation, wealth creation, and the pursuit of knowledge. Ideas flowed freely, and the atmosphere was charged with the excitement of unlimited potential.

Wolf, now a revered figure, shared insights into the interconnectedness of time and the power of embracing both the past and the future. His words resonated with the crowd, inspiring them to dream big and reach for new heights.

The Thanksgiving celebration became a moment of reflection, gratitude, and aspiration. It was a time when the people of Plymouth came together not only to enjoy the bounties of their present but also to envision a future where wealth, knowledge, and love knew no bounds. The table became a place of inspiration, where the limitless possibilities of their interconnected world became a reality.

Within the blanket of time, woven threads so fine, Pilgrims, Wampanoag, in harmony entwine. A Thanksgiving journey, a continuum untold, from Mayflower's deck to futures yet to unfold. Plymouth's echoes whisper through the ages, Wampanoag wisdom, Pilgrim's courageous pages. Modern hearts join the chorus, a harmonious song, together we stand, united, strong.

From feathered quills to digital scrolls, our stories merge, the narrative unfolds. In the spirit of gratitude, a timeless embrace, we wish all a Thanksgiving filled with grace., A table set where past and present coincide. A feast of unity, diversity in every dish, a celebration transcending temporal wish.

With booms of gratitude across the ages, may our spirits soar as history engages. To the present and future, a heartfelt cheer, Happy Thanksgiving to all, far and near!

About the Author:

Jodi Chow is a wife and mother. Jodi graduated with a Master's Degree from Southern Nazarene University. She was a finance executive before settling down with the love of her life. They share a beautiful daughter and two dogs. When Jodi isn't writing, she enjoys hiking, swimming, playing with her family, and reading.

At the time of this publishing, she has 25 short stories and novels for sale on Barnes and Noble. A few titles include: Grave Digger, Pirate's Booty, Holiday Hell, and others. You can also purchase these on Amazon for Kindle and in paperback. Jodi writes for Kindle Vella every Wednesday and Friday. Please support Jodi's writing journey by purchasing some of her work.